LESSONS: LISA

THE LESSONS SERIES

SHEILA MURDOCK

Copyright © 2021 by Sheila Murdock

All rights reserved.

No part of this book may be reproduced in any form or by any electronic or mechanical means, including information storage and retrieval systems, without written permission from the author, except for the use of brief quotations in a book review.

ALSO AVAILABLE IN PAPERBACK

ALSO BY SHEILA MURDOCK

DIVESTED
Crystal
THE DIVESTED BWWM SERIES
SHEILA MURDOCK
The Vain Society
SHEILA MURDOCK
Entitled Woman
SHEILA MURDOCK
LAVONNE ON THE JOB
The Hair Salon
SHEILA MURDOCK
HIS Mess HIS Stress
A NOVEL
SHEILA MURDOCK
LESSONS Lust
SHEILA MURDOCK
Billionaire Bliss
SHEILA MURDOCK
THE Club
A NOVEL
SHEILA MURDOCK
STANDALONES and STANDALONE SERIES
MORE to COME!

NIGHT SKY AFFAIR: TABITHA IS COMING SOON IN 2024

STANDALONES

MORE to COME!

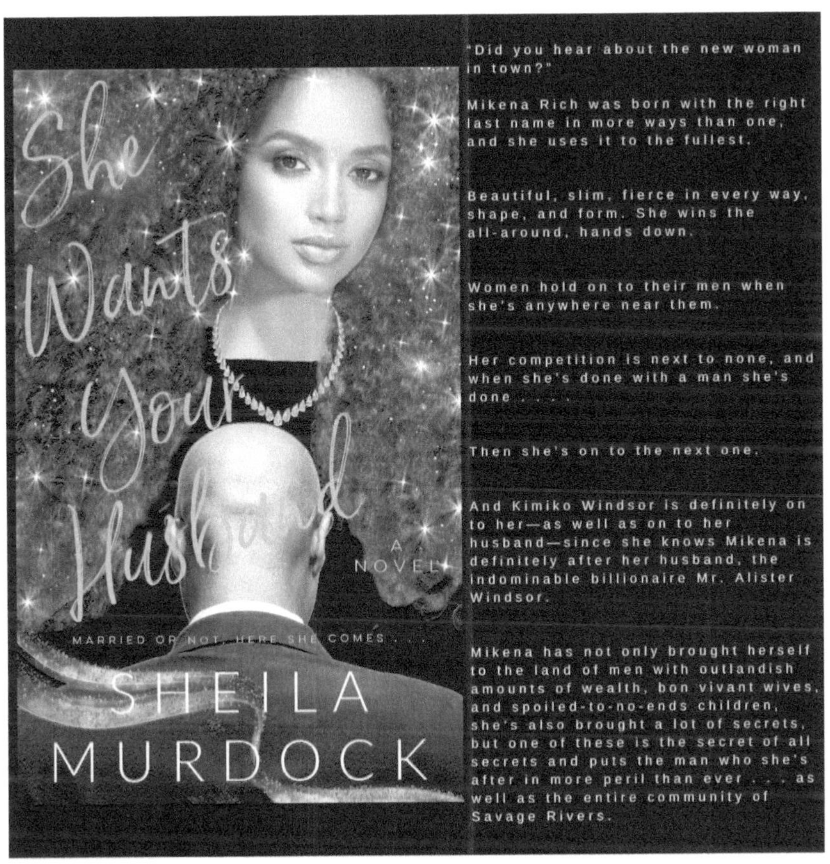

"Did you hear about the new woman in town?"

Mikena Rich was born with the right last name in more ways than one, and she uses it to the fullest.

Beautiful, slim, fierce in every way, shape, and form. She wins the all-around, hands down.

Women hold on to their men when she's anywhere near them.

Her competition is next to none, and when she's done with a man she's done . . . .

Then she's on to the next one.

And Kimiko Windsor is definitely on to her—as well as on to her husband—since she knows Mikena is definitely after her husband, the indominable billionaire Mr. Alister Windsor.

Mikena has not only brought herself to the land of men with outlandish amounts of wealth, bon vivant wives, and spoiled-to-no-ends children, she's also brought a lot of secrets, but one of these is the secret of all secrets and puts the man who she's after in more peril than ever . . . . as well as the entire community of Savage Rivers.

SHE WANTS YOUR HUSBAND - COMING SOON

AUTHOR'S NOTE

LESSONS

The Lessons series is a standalone series so the books don't have to be read in any particular order.

Enjoy,

Sheila Murdock

You can't go back and change the beginning, but you can start where you are and change the ending.

— C.S. LEWIS

CHAPTER ONE

"Lisa," Greg said, as he softly touched her shoulder since she had her back to him while they laid in bed after making love.

"What?" she replied, but didn't bother to turn towards him.

"What is it?"

She shrugged while staring at their wedding picture on the nightstand. "Nothing. I'm just tired, that's all."

He grinned. "C'mon, Lisa. I know you. You're not tired. Something's been bugging you for a while."

She shrugged once again.

"Look at me."

She sighed as she turned and looked at him.

"What's wrong? And don't say nothing, okay? Because I don't believe you."

"I know you don't believe me, Greg, but I just don't wanna talk about it, okay?"

"Well, we need to talk about it some time, so the best time I think would be now."

She turned back over; he turned her back towards him. "I don't wanna talk."

"Well, too bad because we're gonna talk. I'm sick of this shit with you, Lisa. You haven't been yourself for a while. I'm your husband. I know it doesn't seem like I'm around that much, but I do come home every night when I'm not out of town on business or whatever, and you know I don't ignore you when I'm here. Is it because you haven't gotten pregnant yet?"

"I just wish everyone would stay out of our business about it. It's just easier for some women to get pregnant than it is for others. I'm just tired of trying, that's all. Maybe it wasn't meant to be."

"Don't ever say that. I don't even wanna hear that kind of talk. This is gonna happen for us, it has to. I got checked and there are no problems with me, and you got checked out and there are no problems with you, so it's just unexplainable right now, but I know this will happen for us, it will."

She nodded with a smile. "I know it will, honey. I'm just tired of sitting around here all day is all. I have way too much time on my hands. I don't have it all like that where I can do whatever I want like some women can."

"I beg to differ with that, Lisa. You live better than all of your family and friends and most women in this world. You're definitely one of the lucky ones."

"Yeah, well, if I'm so lucky—we're so lucky—how come everyone is able to have a child or multiple children and we're not able to have even one yet?"

"Because everyone is different, okay? But this will happen for us —like I said, it has to. But in the meantime, if you're bored, why don't you get a job?"

"I thought you didn't want me to work? I thought you said I never had to work?" she asked as she started to get angry. "Is there something you're not telling me? We're having money problems that you haven't told me about?"

"No, Lisa, it's nothing like that; not at all. I make well over six figures a year—high six figures—so the last thing we need to worry about is money. It was just a suggestion; don't blow a gasket."

She stared up at the ceiling while still lying in bed. "I'm not." *I'm just not happy,* she thought. She got up out of bed and went into the bathroom and shut the door and locked it.

A knock on the door startled her.

"Lisa! Your phone is ringing!" Greg shouted through the door.

She quickly opened the door as he handed her the phone. It was her best friend, Chassy. "Hey, girl, what's up?"

"Hey, girl. I hope I wasn't interrupting anything," she said.

Lisa glanced at Greg. "No, we're done."

Greg smirked as he put on his pajama pants. "I'm gonna go do some work."

"Okay, don't work too hard," she said.

He left the room and went to his den.

She closed the door behind him. "So, what's going on?"

"Is Greg out of the room?"

"Yeah, he went to go do some work. What's going on?"

"Well, I know I shouldn't be calling you about this because I know you don't care at all, but guess who filed for divorce?"

She shrugged. "I have no idea. Who?"

"Nigel Foreman!" she said with excitement.

"Nigel Foreman? Are you serious? I mean, I don't care because I'm married."

"But I'm not!"

They laughed.

"Yes, girl! Nigel and Aisha are calling it quits after fifteen years of marriage! The High-Nine-Figure Man is gonna be single once again!"

"Actually, I'm surprised their marriage lasted as long as it did. Maybe she got tired of his shit. You can tell how much of an asshole he is. He acts as if he's a billionaire; he's still far from it."

"But he's closer than any other man of any race will ever be to it! Girl, I need to lose this weight and get myself right once again. I wanna be leveled up as much as possible to have a chance with him!"

"Why, Chassy? The guy has a ton of baggage and you have children as well even though you're not married. I wouldn't go after a man like him, seriously, there are way too many better men out there for you. They may not have the high-nine-figure income Nigel has, but at least they're nice men who will respect you. Besides, you said he's filing for divorce, right? It hasn't happened yet."

"No, he *has* filed for divorce, Lisa, you misheard me. Look, I deserve some happiness, okay? I don't have the great life you have, and it's my fault, I'll admit. But how many chances am I gonna get and single women like me to be able to have a chance at Nigel Foreman again? A lot of people thought him and Aisha were never gonna get divorced despite all of his infidelities. He's been with her since high school."

"Well, as you see that doesn't mean anything. People have their reasons for why they feel that things just don't work out after all. Yes, I'm lucky to have been married to Greg since my early twenties and we've been married for ten years and we haven't started our family yet."

"I'm so sorry, Lisa. But you know it will happen, okay? You know I pray for you to get pregnant all the time."

"Thanks, Chassy, I appreciate it. But you know my life is not perfect with Greg. We have our problems and as you see, me not being able to get pregnant is one of them, but I know it will happen."

"I know it will, too. So, I was gonna ask since I got my child support check from my second baby daddy today as well as my work paycheck, did you wanna go out tomorrow and talk about this some more? My treat."

"Well, I don't feel that there's anything to talk about, Chassy. I really don't suggest you try and talk to a man who's not officially divorced yet. I just don't have a good feeling about it."

"I'm not gonna try and talk to Nigel, Lisa . . . I'm gonna wait until he talks to me!"

"Chassy!"

They laughed.

"So, are we on for tomorrow afternoon at our usual spot?"

"How about we go somewhere different? I'm tired of going there."

"Fine with me, but you think of the place."

"No problem."

"So, Nigel Foreman is gonna be a free man once again?" Greg asked, as he looked at his computer while they both laid back in bed for the night.

"Yes, and Chassy is going nuts about it as well as millions of other women, but the bottom line is that he's not officially divorced yet, so I told her not to try and talk to him."

"That's some damn good advice because you don't know how long divorces can take to settle. She doesn't wanna be caught up in that mess with all of those other women, considering the fact that he has nine kids and four of them are by three different women that he fathered outside of his fifteen-year marriage. I'm not a woman but I just don't think it's worth it."

"It's not and Chassy damn well knows it. She shouldn't even be this excited about it. She should wait until he's officially divorced and then try and talk to him, but he's the type who probably won't get married again but will have a bunch of girlfriends."

"Like I heard he did all throughout his marriage."

"I know. If he didn't respect Aisha what makes her think he's gonna respect her if there's a one percent chance she ends up in a serious relationship with him?"

"He's not. He's proven that. Men like him will never be faithful. He's got tremendous wealth and with that comes power and privilege. He doesn't seem like a nice guy, either, so I don't understand why so many women are already lining up to be the next Mrs. Foreman."

"Well, you listed the reasons why they're lining up, Greg, and that's all that matters. And you know she wants to meet with me tomorrow to talk about this some more?"

"She loves to dream and gossip, huh?"

"Ever since I've known her!" she laughed. "I just don't see the point in this, but if this is something she wants to talk about then it's my job as her best friend to listen."

"Now that's being a good best friend," he said with a smile. "Let me know how it goes. I can't wait to hear all about it."

CHAPTER TWO

"Wow, this is a nice place you picked out, Lisa," Chassy said, as they sat inside a gourmet bakery shop that specialized in serving too-pretty-to-eat sweet treats along with coffee and other specialty drinks. "Where did you find it?"

"I've been here a few times by myself when I felt a sweet attack coming on, as well as to get gifts for family and friends. I did get you something from here for your birthday a few years ago and you don't even remember?"

Chassy hung her head in shame. "No, I don't remember, Lisa. Sorry. You know I got four kids to take care of, so I forget what even happened yesterday."

"But you didn't forget about Nigel Foreman, did you? That's why you wanted to go out with me today to talk about him. And I thought this was a nice place to talk. I love the beautiful, fancy feminine atmosphere."

"Yeah, it's beautiful, but everything is too expensive for me personally."

"Well, now, you can't back out since you said it was your treat," she reminded her with a grin.

Chassy grinned back. "I know, so I'm glad you didn't get too crazy." She looked out the window since they sat right by one. "Speaking about crazy, what is going on out there?"

Lisa looked out the window as well. "I don't know, but we'll find out—or you tell me because I gotta go use the bathroom."

"Okay, go on," Chassy said, as her eyes were glued to the outside.

Minutes later, Lisa returned to find the shop almost completely crowded with women as they surrounded no other than Nigel Foreman!

I have to admit, he's gorgeous in person, she thought, since this was her first time actually seeing him in person. She looked over at Chassy as she now sat on the edge of her seat getting pictures and videos just like what almost everyone in the shop was doing, which pretty much made him a celebrity just because of his staggering wealth.

"Oh, my God, Lisa! Can you freakin' believe this? Am I dreaming? Is Nigel Foreman really in this shop?"

"Yeah, he's really in this shop. I instantly recognized him. I've never seen him in person," she replied with a smile. "Well, I seemed to have picked this place for a reason, Chassy, so go on over there and get all of those women off of him and claim your soon-to-be-divorced man."

"Now I'm so nervous, Lisa! I don't think I can do it! I never thought in a million years I would see him in person this fast, and just think, we were gonna go to our usual spot today. I'm so glad you chose this spot!"

"I knew there was a reason why I chose it as well," she replied with a smile.

"IF YOU'RE NOT IN HERE TO ORDER ANYTHING THEN YOU NEED TO LEAVE," the shop's owner informed people in an annoyed voice.

"I don't blame her," Lisa said, as she still watched the Nigel mob all around him, men and women.

"She knows they're all in here because of Nigel. And, girl, he pulled up in that beautiful black Bugatti right there! Damn! I'm seeing myself in that car right now!"

"You're not gonna see yourself in anything if you don't go over there and try and talk to him, Chassy. I'm serious. Here's your chance. I know I shouldn't be encouraging this, but us coming here instead of our usual spot and at this time happened for a reason, so don't blow this chance."

"I know," she said, and took a deep breath. "Okay, I'll go talk to him . . . but I gotta use the bathroom first since I'm so nervous! Be right back!" She jumped up and quickly went to the bathroom.

Lisa chuckled as she looked at her phone, not wanting to pay attention to what everyone else was paying attention to. She began to text Greg about Chassy's chance happening . . . .

"Hi."

She looked up from her phone.

Nigel Foreman was staring down at her with a smile!

She almost dropped her phone as she stared up at him in shock. "Hi," she finally replied.

"I'm Nigel Foreman," he replied with a smile as he extended his hand out.

"Lisa Everett," she replied as she shook hands with him.

"Is this seat taken?" he asked.

"Yes, it is. My best friend is sitting there. She's in the bathroom right now."

"Well, I don't wanna take her seat then. I've never seen you here before."

"I don't come here that often since it's out of the way, but I order a lot online."

He nodded with a smile. "It's one of my daughter's favorite spots. I was just picking up something for her." He checked his watch. "Can I give you a call sometime?"

"Sure, that will be fine," she replied with a smile, and gave him her number.

"Great, Lisa. I'll call you tonight."

"Okay."

Less than a minute later, she watched as his entourage of friends and fans all followed him out of the bakery and to his car.

Chassy returned from the bathroom minutes later. "Damnit! He's freakin' gone! I knew I shouldn't have taken that long in there! I thought he was gonna be in here longer. Oh, well. I follow him on social media so I can see if he posts next where he's gonna be or whatever, so all is definitely not lost," she said, and then took a bite of her cupcake and then sipped on her coffee.

Lisa continued to stare out the window in total shock at something she never thought would happen . . . and knew she could never tell her best friend.

"Thanks for surprising me with my favorite, baby. What's the occasion?" Greg asked, as they sat down for dinner later that evening.

"No occasion," Lisa replied with a smile. "I just thought I'd make you your favorite since I haven't made it in a while."

"Well, I appreciate it," he replied with a smile and then started eating his lasagna. "So, I see Nigel Foreman was at the bakery that you and Chassy where at this afternoon, huh?"

"Yeah, what are the odds of that happening?" she said, and then ate some of her salad. "I picked the place since I was tired of going to our usual spot, and he happened to be there when I walked out of the bathroom. I knew Chassy was gonna post that video everywhere of him being in there, but then she got cold feet and went to the bathroom and by the time she got out of it, he was gone."

He laughed. "Just like that that, huh?"

"Yeah, just like that."

He continued to stare at her. "So, neither one of you met him? Especially Chassy?"

"No," she lied. "I stayed in my seat the whole time. How would I have looked jumping up like some desperate woman wanting to be all around him and totally crowding his space like those other women were doing when he was just there to pick up something for one of his daughters?"

"And how did you know that?"

She felt herself go into a panic. "Because Chassy told me. She heard him say it while he was there," she lied. "And he probably has it written on his social media pages since he's on there a lot, I heard."

"Yeah, probably, but I don't follow him."

"And neither do I," she honestly replied.

"Well, I hope Chassy realizes that a man like that is not worth pursuing, especially since he's not legally divorced yet. The most he would've probably got was her number and said he would call her and never would. I know how men are."

"Yeah, you're right. But they're not all like that."

"But most are. I hate to say this about Chassy since she's your best friend, but she's a baby mama to four kids by two different men. Men like Nigel wouldn't even look at her if he knew that about her. Nigel is the type that likes women who are readily available to him and who are beautiful and in shape, not average looking with a bunch of kids and out of shape like Chassy. Hate to say it, but it's true."

"You're mean," she said with a grin.

"The truth hurts," he replied as he returned the grin, and took a sip of his red wine.

Her phone rang.

Nigel.

Greg looked at her. "Who is it?"

"Spam," she lied, and turned her phone off. "I forgot to turn my phone off. You know our rules and I broke them. Sorry."

"It's okay. You're not gonna remember to turn it off all the time," he replied as he held a look of skepticism.

.   .   .

Lisa peeked in on Greg in his den while he talked on the phone to one of his friends while typing something on his computer. She headed downstairs and into the garage where her car was parked. She climbed inside and called Nigel back.

"Hello?"

"Hey, Nigel."

"Who is this?" he asked.

"Um, it's Lisa," she said in confusion.

"Lisa who? I know a lot of Lisas."

"Lisa Everett."

"Everett?"

She tried not to sigh. She didn't know now if it was even a good idea to have called him back. "Um, you just called me about a half hour ago, but I was eating dinner and didn't have my phone near me. I'm returning your call."

"Oh, oh yeah. Okay. What's up, baby?"

Well, you called me, she thought. "Not much. I'm just always bored."

"You wanna come over here? I forgot why I called you, but if you wanna come over here it's cool. I'm all alone."

She looked at the garage door to see if Greg was gonna come out of it. "Um, sure. Where do you live?"

He gave her his address. "Oh, and I'll let the guard at the front gate know you're coming over. When should I expect you?"

"In about an hour. I just need to freshen up."

"Cool. See you then."

Minutes later, she stood outside of Greg's den as he still talked on his phone while looking at something on his computer.

He looked up at her. "Just a minute, man," he said. "What is it, Lisa?"

"I'm gonna go see Chassy. She just got into a big fight with her first baby daddy over child support."

"Again?" he said. "Damn, she should've chose better, but too late now. And she thinks a man like Nigel Foreman is gonna sweep her off of her feet and take her away from all of her mess?"

"Come on, Greg, be nice. She's my best friend; she needs me."

"She needs a psychologist and birth control."

"Greg!" she said with a chuckle.

"It's true. Just let me know when you get there and when you're coming back."

"As always, I will."

CHAPTER THREE

Lisa stared in amazement at the jaw-dropping front guard-gated entry to this exclusive community. Even though she felt she lived a privileged life, there were very few entries to homes that could top this. She nervously waited in line since there was a car in front of her with a person talking to the guard. She watched as the gates opened and the car was let through, and then closed once again.

"May I help you?" the mean-looking guard asked as if he was irritated all day by people coming in and out of the community.

"Yes, I'm here to see Nigel Foreman."

The guard nodded and typed something on his computer. "What is your name?"

"Lisa Everett," she replied in a nervous tone.

He continued to look at his computer. "I see Lisa, but no Everett," he informed her.

She didn't know what to say. "Um, I just talked to him no more than an hour ago. He should be expecting me."

He got on his phone. "Mr. Foreman? Front gate. Are you expecting a Lisa Everett? . . . Everett, that's right. Okay." He hung up. "Go on."

"Thank you," she said as she tried not to breathe a sigh of relief in front of him.

The gates slowly opened, and she made her way into one of the most beautiful and most exclusive communities she'd ever been in. Each house she passed she knew was well over several million dollars. This was the ultimate life, whether it be new money or old money, and Nigel Foreman was a combination of both.

She arrived at his house where the front gates to it were opened. She slowly drove up the driveway and stared in complete awe at the size of his house. It was nothing like she'd ever seen before in her life. She parked her car and was about to get out when she saw another woman leaving his house!

She quickly ducked out of sight, forgetting that the windows were tinted on her brand-new black Maserati Levante SUV, a ten-year anniversary gift from her husband. She looked up in her rearview mirror and saw the woman get into her car and leave. She had no idea who she was, but she knew it wasn't Aisha, Nigel's soon-to-be ex-wife.

She sat in her car for another minute as she tried to figure out what she was doing here after all. She knew she hadn't done anything wrong by just meeting up with a man who invited her over . . . but this was no ordinary man. This was a well-known man of great wealth who announced to the world that him and his wife were getting a divorce . . . but they weren't officially divorced yet, and as a married woman, she knew the only thing that could come out of a relationship with Nigel was just being friends *if* Greg would let it happen, but she didn't count on it.

She finally got out of the car and nervously walked up to his home. She rang the doorbell as she took in the beautiful, majestic view. She couldn't believe that she was here.

"Hey," Nigel said with a smile, while being shirtless with a pair of light blue jeans on.

"Hi," she replied with a smile, as she stared at his amazing chiseled six-pack abs and beautiful muscular arms that were full of tattoos. He not only had the wealth in dollars, but in his health as well.

"Come on in."

She walked in and felt she'd stepped into a royal palace. "Wow, your home is absolutely beautiful. It's stunning."

"Thank you, baby. Old money and new money combined and this is the result of it. You want anything to drink?"

"No thank you, I'm driving."

"That's cool. Let's go into the rec room. I was watching TV."

Obviously with that woman who left when I got here, she thought.

Minutes later, they were in the rec room staring at a basketball game on his 100-inch TV.

"You sure you don't want anything to drink?"

"Just a bottle of water."

"You got it." He gave her the bottle.

"Thank you," she replied with a nervous tone.

He kept staring at her as he sat on a chair adjacent to the couch she was sitting on. "Are you nervous about something?"

"No, not at all," she lied. "I was just wondering who the woman was that I saw leaving at the same time I pulled up in your driveway. I thought you were alone."

"Yeah, we are now. She's just some chick I fuck once in a while. Nothing serious."

"Oh, okay," she replied. *Just as I suspected,* she thought. "Um, so, you and your wife are getting a divorce? I hate to ask but it's been everywhere in the media."

"If that's what was said then yeah, it's gonna happen. We should've never gotten married. I only did it to protect her and my kid—the one she was pregnant with as to the reason why we got married to begin with. We ended up having four more together, but marriage is not for me, and it took me fifteen years to realize it but hey, better late than never."

"It isn't for everyone, that's for sure," she said, and then changed the subject. "You know? My best friend has the biggest crush on you.

As you know, she was in the bathroom at the shop today when you talked to me."

He smiled. "Really? Well, I only saw you sitting there and you looked so beautiful but lonely." He continued to stare at her. "Are you lonely, Lisa?"

She sighed as she tried not to get emotional. "Yes, I have to admit it. I am. I'm just so bored with everything. I feel like I've done everything many times over but then again I feel like my life hasn't even begun yet."

"Do you have children?"

"No, I don't. Maybe that's what's missing, I don't know. I'm in no way in a rush to have them, though."

"How old are you?"

"36," she replied.

"Yeah, you have a few more years, but don't wait too long, and you don't wanna have as many as I have. Even though I can afford them, it's a whole other thing raising them. Luckily, I had my soon-to-be ex-wife so we raised them together, and even though they're young, it doesn't get easier."

"I'll keep that in mind," she replied with a smile.

"So, is there anything you would like to do while you're here?"

This question caught her off guard and sounded very suggestive.

"Um, I didn't have anything particular in mind, so anything you want since it's your house."

He grinned as he sat back in his chair and stared at her, and then turned his attention back to the game. His phone rang. "Hey, what's up, man? . . . Yeah, I'm alone."

She looked at him . . . and immediately felt disrespected. She watched as he got up and went to the bar and made himself a drink. She sat quietly on the couch as he continued to talk to his friend as if he was all alone. She remembered when she called him that he told her he was alone, but it was clear he wasn't and it was proven by the woman who'd left his house when she was in the driveway.

What in the world am I really doing here? she thought.

Her phone rang. It was Greg. She went into a panic and turned off her ringer as Nigel looked at her since he'd heard her phone ring. He turned his back on her as he still carried on a conversation with one of his friends leaving her still feeling all alone.

Her phone chimed in with a text:

You didn't tell me when you got to Chassy's. I know you're there by now.

I am. She's okay now so I'm about to leave. See you when I get home.

Okay, baby. Be safe.

"Um, Nigel?"

"Yeah, what's up?" he asked, and then took a sip of his drink while he was still on the phone.

"I gotta go."

"Okay, let me walk you to the door."

At home comfortably in her pajamas, and with Greg still working in his den, she decided to do an entry in her diary that she had on her computer:

I can't believe I did this. Yes, I went to go see him after knowing him for only a few hours, but I didn't do what most women would've done if they went to his house. Didn't happen. Every woman wants to be with him, but for some reason he noticed me and only me in the shop today. He asked me for my number so I gave it to him; didn't see any harm in it. Chassy still doesn't know I actually met him and neither does Greg—but it doesn't matter. I don't think I will be seeing him again.

Greg walked into the room; she closed her computer. "You don't have to stop looking at porn just because I walked into the room."

"Greg!" she said as she threw her nail filer at him. "I don't look at that smut. I was just browsing at a clothing store."

He laughed. "I know you don't, baby." He climbed into bed with her. "It's been a long day. I hope your day was better than mine."

"It was okay. Nothing out of the ordinary," she lied. "Goodnight, honey."

"Goodnight, baby."

He turned over and was asleep within minutes, but she couldn't sleep. She stared up at the ceiling as she thought about the day she had today, and knew that even though she didn't do anything over at Nigel's house, the whole thing just didn't sit right with her, so she had to talk to someone other than Chassy about it.

CHAPTER FOUR

C‍HASSY MAY HAVE BEEN HER BEST FRIEND, BUT S‍HARITA WAS L‍ISA'S BEST AND favorite cousin, someone who was always there to listen to her problems and disclose her deepest, darkest secrets to, and most of all, told her things she didn't want Chassy to know.

"So, I'm the only who knows you met Nigel Foreman, huh?" Sharita said with a grin, as she and Lisa sat in her kitchen indulging in fresh fruit and coffee.

"Yeah, you're the only one who knows. I honestly don't know why Chassy has this big crush on him. If she knew more about him then she probably wouldn't like him at all."

"What is it about him that you don't like?"

"Well, I don't like the fact that he said to a friend of his that he was alone when the friend called him. He wasn't alone. I was sitting right there in his rec room on the couch watching TV with him. He didn't have to say who I was, just the fact that he did have company. I felt disrespected, I can't lie. And when the friend called, he got up and made himself a drink and it's like he forgot that I was even there.

"Greg had called me when he was still talking to his friend and he heard my phone ring because he looked at me in curiosity. I just texted Greg back and said that Chassy was okay and that I was coming home since I lied to him and told him that's where I was going. I just felt so bad lying like that, Sharita. And not only that, but using Chassy in the process since she really likes Nigel. I just wish there was some way I could tell her that she should just forget about him."

"Why? Because you already have something going on with him?"

"I have *nothing* going on with him, Sharita, you know that. I'm married."

"Does he know you're married?"

She paused. It now hit her. Something that she didn't even think about. She sighed and shook her head. "No, he doesn't. He didn't even ask me."

"That's because he doesn't care if you are or not."

"You think so?"

"I know so, Lisa. Nigel is the type of man who doesn't care about a woman's education, marital status—even though he's in the process of getting a divorce—what she does for a living, nothing. All he cares about is her beauty, body, and being submissive to him and not having any children even though he has nine of them—but it's not about him since he has all the wealth so that means he has all the power, and he's said this a lot on social media since I follow him. It was clear that he was attracted to you, Lisa, otherwise he would've never came up to you in the shop yesterday."

"Well, I can't disagree with that. I was just surprised that he did come up to me. He said I looked lonely sitting there, even though Chassy was in the bathroom. She had her chance to talk to him and she didn't."

"Please, someone like Nigel Foreman does not want a woman like Chassy. Hate to say it like that since she's your best friend and all, but it's true."

Lisa grinned. "Greg said the same thing. But you know since she is my best friend, I can't tell her what you both have said."

"You don't have to because she'll find out soon enough. So, what else did he ask you?"

"He asked me how old I was, did I have any children, and if I was lonely."

"And what did you say?"

"I told him I didn't have any children and that I was lonely because I am, I'm not gonna lie. I just don't know what to do more than half the time now. Like I told him last night, I feel like I've done everything many times over, but at the same time I feel as if my life hasn't even begun yet."

"Wait till you have your first child," she said with a smile.

"Please don't start on that. You know I've never told Greg this, but I'm just not sure if having kids is a hundred percent for me."

"Really? Then you really need to talk to him about this, Lisa. Everyone's experience is different and no one, and I mean absolutely no one, is a hundred percent ready for it. I know I wasn't, and I have three. But you know how much I envy you because Greg married you and you didn't have to have any kids before he did because he truly loves you. I just don't think my man is ever gonna ask me to marry him."

"Well, don't give up hope, Sharita. But then again, you'll know when the time is right to move on."

"Yeah, sometimes I wish I would meet a Nigel Foreman, but men like that are way out of my league. I know who I *don't* qualify for, and he's definitely the type."

"Well, I'm gonna be honest with you about him, Sharita. He doesn't seem to be that nice of a person. When he first called me yesterday, I was having dinner with Greg. I called him back almost a half hour later and it's like he forgot he met me yesterday."

"For real?"

"Yeah, for real."

"He meets a lot of women, Lisa, so that doesn't surprise me. But he should know who he gives his number to."

"I know. And it's like I felt like hanging up right there. I just kept saying to myself why the hell am I doing this, you know? I'm married. Why did I exchange numbers with a man when I know damn well I'm married—but he didn't and still doesn't know I am, and like you said, it's clear that he doesn't care either way. Am I really that bored and lonely that I want some more excitement in my life and I feel that being friends with a man like Nigel will give me what I feel I'm missing?"

Sharita continued to stare at her. "Only you know the answers to everything you're saying, Lisa. I just hope you make the right choices because too many of us have made the wrong ones."

"Hey, I haven't always made good choices. I'm not perfect."

"I know. But some choices have detrimental consequences. If you wanna keep seeing him in a way that won't mean any harm to your marriage, go ahead, I don't see anything wrong with it. But please, make the choices that you know are the right ones. Just because this guy has almost a billion dollars doesn't mean he's the right choice for most women. He wouldn't be getting a divorce from Aisha if he was really a good choice."

"That's true. Since I'm married, I shouldn't care if he's getting a divorce like all of the other women who care."

"Honestly, you really shouldn't. Let him have his fun with those other desperate women. You have a great husband, something they wish they had and me as well."

She smiled. "I do."

"I can't believe my second baby daddy wants me to give him another chance!" Chassy said as she and Lisa talked on the phone later on that evening.

"Well, I think you should, Chassy. You need to have some stability for the sake of yourself and for your kids. Even though he's the father of the youngest ones, it will be nice for him to be a role model for your two oldest kids."

"And that's what he said he would like to be, and they're cool with it. I mean, what other choices do I have?"

"Well, if there's anyone you should be with it should definitely be with at least one of your children's fathers. This will show them that things can work out after all. And personally, I like him more than the first baby daddy."

"I know, Lisa, you always have. So, I guess I can say that I'm willing to work this out with him because a man should be in the house when you have children. You've had a man in the house for ten years and you don't have any kids yet."

"And I don't know if I ever will, but we're not talking about me, we're talking about you. So, what about Nigel Foreman?" she asked with a grin.

"Oh, you know a girl can always dream, right? And that's all that it was, a dream. I don't think a man like Nigel will ever be interested in me. If he really was then we would've met yesterday at the shop. It's clear he likes women that are the opposite of me, but that's okay because I'm working it out with my second baby daddy. Having someone is better than having no one."

"That's true, but you want that someone to be someone that's worth being with, so I'm genuinely glad that you are working things out with him."

Greg came into the room. "I need to talk to you right now."

She looked at him in curiosity. "About what?"

"Hang up right now. I mean it."

"Um, Chassy, I gotta go. Talk to you tomorrow."

"Okay, girl."

She sighed while she still stayed where she was. "What is it?"

He came by her and stood over her with his phone in his hand. "Mind explaining this to me?" He gave her his phone that showed Nigel talking to her in the bakery! They were caught in the background of a woman's selfie!

"I can explain it, Greg."

"I'm listening," he replied as he still stood over her while glaring down at her.

"I was completely minding my business looking at my phone. Someone said hi to me and I looked up and there he was, standing over me like the way you are right now. He just said I looked lonely sitting there, obviously trying to make conversation with me. He even asked me was the seat Chassy was sitting in taken and I said it was hers and that she was in the bathroom. Nothing else happened."

He sighed. "Then if nothing else happened then why didn't you tell me that you met him? You told me the two of you saw him there, but you didn't tell me you met him."

"Because I didn't think it was important, and if I'd mentioned it then you would've gotten mad like how you are now."

He looked at the picture once again and then turned his phone off. He sat on the bed beside her. "I'm not mad, Lisa. I'm just surprised that you left this part out of it. I don't care at all that you met him, okay? It was obviously a chance happening; I believe you. He came up to you because you're beautiful and he probably thought you were single. You told him you're married, right?"

"Yes, I told him," she lied.

"And that makes me feel good," he said with a smile. He kissed her on the cheek.

But she'd never felt so bad. She believed Sharita when she'd told her that men like Nigel did not care whether or not a woman was married, and she knew if she decided that she wanted to see him again that she'd better tell him because the longer she withheld the truth, the worse it was going to be.

"Well, I'm gonna go do some work. Talk to you later," he said.

"Okay," she replied with a smile.

They kissed.

A minute later, she received a text:

Are you lonely tonight?

Nigel.

She sighed. She knew what he wanted, and she felt that she'd better tell him that she was married since he didn't know. She texted him back:

Not lonely, just tired. I'm about to go to bed early.
Okay, cool. Goodnight, beautiful.
Goodnight, Nigel.

She got on her computer to write an entry in her diary:

Greg found out that I really did meet Nigel yesterday at the bakery. He was upset about it and asked me if I'd told him I was married. I lied and said that I did. He didn't ask me did we exchange numbers. I think telling him that I did tell Nigel that I was married made him automatically think that we didn't exchange numbers. And Nigel just texted me a minute ago asking me if I was lonely tonight. I told him I wasn't even though I am. I just don't wanna hurt Greg, that's all. I know he would not allow me to see Nigel even as a friend—there's always something about it, especially since Nigel has a lot of wealth which always equates to having power and prestige. But I do need to tell Nigel that I'm just not available for him to wanna see to do whatever with. He's not even legally divorced yet so any way you look at it, neither one of us really have any business seeing each other other than just being friends, but I believe just being friends is the last thing he has in mind.

And I don't have to worry about Chassy's obsessive love for Nigel anymore. She's gonna give her second baby daddy a second chance. She even admitted that she has no realistic chance with Nigel, but I still don't feel comfortable with her knowing that I did meet him yesterday, and I especially don't want her knowing that I went over his house as well. I just don't know how she would feel about me if she found all of this out, and I don't even wanna think about it if Greg found out that I was at his house last night.

But Nigel has the right to know I'm married even if it's true that he doesn't care either way, and I just can't keep putting this off any longer.

CHAPTER FIVE

It was date night tonight for Lisa and Greg, date number two of the three they had for the month. Lisa really looked forward to it since this was a night she didn't have to cook because they always went out to eat at the restaurant of her choice, but when she couldn't decide, Greg suggested one, and that was what he did for this night.

"So, you can't stop your love for Italian food, huh?" she said with a smile as she looked at her menu.

"It's my favorite type of food. Nothing wrong with a black man loving Italian food," he replied as he looked at his menu as well. "You know I will always choose it if you don't know where you want to go for the night."

"It's always fine with me," she said. "So, how was your day today?"

"It was fine, honey. But if you don't mind, I don't wanna talk about my day."

"Okay, what do you wanna talk about?"

He sighed, and then took a sip of his water. "Well, I just wanna know how you're truly doing, Lisa. I feel that I'm here enough for you, but I know it's been hard for us since we're still trying for our first child, it's just—"

"I don't wanna talk about this, Greg, not here. This is supposed to be our date night. This is a night where we're not supposed to be fighting and talking about things that we know will upset us."

"But I can't help it, Lisa. I feel like you're disconnecting from me for some reason and I just can't have that happen."

"I'm not disconnecting from you, Greg. Now I feel that you're trying to hide something from me."

"I'm not hiding anything from you, Lisa, not a damn thing. But I'm not gonna lie, you meeting Nigel is still getting to me."

"And why is that, Greg?"

"Because I don't think you're being honest with me about him."

She tried not to gasp. She tried to control her breathing. "What am I not being honest about?"

"Come on, Lisa. Nigel Foreman? He comes up to you in a shop and you haven't spoken to him since?"

"And what are you trying to say?"

"That I know the two of you exchanged contact info, *that's* what I'm trying to say."

"You can't prove that we did," she said as she tried not get angry.

"I just did," he replied.

"How?"

"Because you never said you didn't," he replied.

She sighed as she looked around the restaurant. "Why are you trying to pick a fight here, Greg? If you wanted to talk about all of this then we could've just stayed home, ordered from Grubhub or Door-Dash, and talked about this. This is not the place to do it."

He looked to his left. "Looks like this is the perfect place to do it."

"What are you looking—"

She looked his way . . . .

And Nigel walked into the restaurant with two of his friends!

Nigel immediately recognized Lisa as him and his friends were seated at a table across the restaurant and directly in their view.

Greg smirked as he shook his head. "Did you know he was gonna be here tonight? Because you did post on social media that we had a date night tonight and gave the name of this restaurant. And since there's only one like this in the city, everyone knows where it is."

"I guess I have to stop putting so much info on there," she said, and then shielded herself from Nigel's view with her menu.

"No use in trying to hide from him, Lisa. He knows it's you."

She sighed as she put the menu down. She looked right into Nigel's eyes. "Um, where's the waiter? I'm ready to order."

Several minutes later their food arrived . . . as well as an expensive bottle of red wine.

"I didn't order this," Greg said.

"It's complimentary from the High-Nine-Figure Man, Nigel Foreman," the waiter said.

"Take it back, we don't need his complimentary anything. I take care of myself and my wife just fine."

"Greg!" Lisa said. "That's rude as hell to refuse a bottle of wine from someone who is paying for it."

"It's not when I know he's trying to clown me in front of you, and he's not gonna do it."

"Very well, sir," the waiter said, and took the bottle of wine away. He walked over to Nigel's table and told him that it was refused. He nodded as his friends shook their heads.

Lisa stared at Nigel while Greg ate his food as if he wasn't there. *"I'm sorry,"* she mouthed to him.

Nigel nodded in response and continued talking to his friends.

"You know, you really embarrassed me tonight by refusing that bottle of wine," Lisa said as they drove home from the restaurant.

"Don't even start with me, Lisa. If anything, he was trying to embarrass me by doing that shit, and I wasn't having it. And our waiter had a nerve to say 'High-Nine-Figure Man' before his name? What kind of shit is that?"

"Well, he's one of the very few black men in this world who makes that kind of money so that's what he's known for."

"That and a hell of a lot of other things that are more bad than good. He's not even officially divorced yet and he's out here trying to show off for women in front of their men. Yeah, I wonder how many other couples he's done that to."

"Why are you making such a big deal out of it?"

"Because it is a big deal, Lisa, so don't sit there and say that it isn't. I don't appreciate him trying to clown me in front of you, and I'm not making any apologies for it. He better be lucky I didn't take that bottle and bust open his head with it for doing that shit."

"And then you would be in jail and your job would be in jeopardy."

"That's why I didn't do it. I kept myself respectable even though I could've been the complete opposite. Nigel needs to know what respect is. I didn't have any problem with the dude until he did that shit tonight. It was nothing about him trying to be friendly or respectable, Lisa, it was about him showing that he had more power than me because he has more money, that's all, and that was completely disrespecting our marriage and me as a man."

"Well, if you put it that way, Greg, it was disrespectful, I'll admit that. But I thought you were gonna do something to him for doing that. I'm glad you showed class, honey."

He smiled. "I had no other choice."

They sat in silence for a second.

"And I don't want you talking to him again, Lisa. I'm your husband, not him. You have enough friends and family you can talk to. I know a toxic dude when I see one, and his money has nothing to do with it."

She continued to stare out the window.

"Did you hear me?" he asked.

"Yes, I heard you."

CHAPTER SIX

"Girl, *everyone* is talking about what happened with y'all and Nigel at the restaurant last night," Sharita said, as she handed Lisa a cup of hot tea.

"Yeah, I'm sure they are. I know Nigel was gonna make a big deal out of it since he posted it on his social media pages, stating that he tried to give a happy-in-love-looking couple an expensive bottle of wine, but we rejected it. No, *Greg* rejected it, not me."

"Well, you knew that was a given, Lisa. Greg really took control last night like a real man does. You really have a great husband, a total alpha male. No real man was gonna let another man clown him like that because he knew why Nigel did that."

"Yeah, that's what he said," she said, and took a sip of her tea. "And he told me later on while we were driving home that he was gonna take that bottle and bust open his head with it, but thought about me and his job."

"And that's just thinking smart on his part." She sighed. "Lisa, do you think Nigel knew you and Greg were going there last night?"

"I don't see how he didn't know. I don't see anything about him following me on any of my social media pages and to be fair, he only follows close friends and family, and the women that he follows are friends and family. Everyone knows that he unfollowed his wife when it was announced that they're getting a divorce. But that doesn't mean he hasn't been looking at my pages."

"Yeah, you're right about that because it's obvious that he has been. But he still didn't know you were married, right?"

"Yeah, but I know he knows now. And I have to admit I should've told him when I first met him. Greg is really pissed off about me lying to him about not telling him that I really did meet him after all. If it wasn't for us being caught talking to each other in the background of that woman's selfie then he would've never known."

"I know, that's fucked up, Lisa. You just never know whose background you're gonna end up in when you're not paying attention."

"And I learned the hard way. Greg also said last night that he doesn't want me talking to him anymore, and remember, he has no idea that I've seen him once since meeting him. I haven't even done anything with Nigel. It's been completely harmless. I feel that I need to talk to him at least one more time to tell him that I'm sorry for Greg rejecting his bottle of wine last night. He really embarrassed me when he did that."

"Oh, I'm sure he did, Lisa, but you know why he did it. I think any man would've done what Greg did so you can't be mad at him for it."

"I'm not mad, I was just embarrassed, that's all."

"Perfectly understandable."

Lisa's phone chimed in with a text. "Oh, my God! It's Nigel!"

"For real?" Sharita said with surprise.

They looked at the text:

I wanna talk to you in person. Are you available right now?

Lisa looked at Sharita. "What should I text back to him?"

She shrugged. "I can't tell you what to do or say, you're a grown woman."

Lisa took a deep breath and texted him back:

Sure, that's fine. We do need to talk. Where do you wanna meet at?

My office right now. I'll give you the address.
Got it. See you there.

"Mr. Foreman will be with you in a few minutes, Mrs. Everett," his secretary said with a smile.

"Thank you," Lisa replied with a smile as she sat in Nigel's luxury spatial office at his construction company. She continued to see just how well he actually lived, and he was a real power producer, making almost all of the new money that made up his family's high-nine-figure fortune.

"Hey, Lisa," Nigel said as he walked in the office and sat in his chair behind his desk.

"Hi, Nigel," she replied with a smile.

They stared at each other in an awkward silence, and it was as if he was waiting for her to say something.

"I just wanna say that I'm sorry for what Greg did to you last night. I told him how much he embarrassed me and himself by doing what he did."

"Is he your husband?"

She lowered her head. "Yes." She looked up at him to find him grinning back at her.

"Doesn't surprise me, Lisa. I knew you being single was probably too good to be true. But how come you didn't tell me when we first met that you had a man? And not only a man, but a husband?"

"I honestly don't know why, Nigel. I guess I was so shocked that you came up to me that day."

"But you knew you were married when I came up to you."

"I know, and I'm sorry I didn't tell you. That was wrong."

"And it's obvious your husband doesn't like me."

"He never said he didn't, he just said that you were trying to clown him."

"I was just being nice."

"I know you were and I tried to tell him that but he didn't believe me. He just said you were showing off in front of us and in front of your friends by doing what you did."

He shrugged. "Well, I was being nice. He can think what he wants to think. I knew who you were and thought I'd do something nice. If it offended him then it offended him. It usually does offend men who aren't on my level."

"Well, hardly any men are on your level, Nigel. I just wanna say I'm sorry for my husband's actions."

"You said it so it's cool. And it's obviously still cool that we're talking like this even though you're married and I'm soon-to-be divorced."

"It is," she said with a smile, as she tried to block out the fact that Greg told her not to talk to him anymore. She looked at her phone. It was Greg. "I have to take this call."

"Go right ahead."

"Hi, honey."

"Hey, baby. I have a little free time in between patients. What's for dinner tonight?"

"I haven't thought about it. Anything you want you know I'll make," she replied as she looked at Nigel as he stared back at her with a huge grin.

"Where are you? You don't sound like you're at home."

"At Sharita's," she lied.

He laughed out loud!

"Who was that?" he asked.

"Her boyfriend," she quickly said in a panic.

"He doesn't laugh like that, Lisa, I know his laugh. Are you really at Sharita's?"

She looked at Nigel as he stared back at her.

"No," she replied.

"Where are you?"

"Out shopping. I decided to stop at Starbucks."

Nigel laughed out loud once again.

"Oh, okay. Well, I gotta get back to work. Make anything you want, baby, you know I'll eat it."

"Okay."

She breathed a sigh of relief after hanging up.

"You don't lie a lot, do you?" he asked as he chuckled.

She sighed as she stared down at her phone. "I have to be honest with you, Nigel."

"About what?"

"Greg doesn't want me talking to you, so I know he especially doesn't want me seeing you."

"Does he know that you've seen me alone once before since we've met? And now twice?"

"No, and I don't want him to know."

He shrugged. "Well, him not wanting you to talk to me anymore is not surprising to me. I know dude doesn't like me; hardly any men do because like I said, hardly any of them are on my level. I'm used to the haters."

"He's not a hater. I told him there's nothing about you he shouldn't like, but he's not trying to hear me."

"Fuck him then," he replied.

She gasped. "He's my husband, Nigel."

"Well, I honestly don't care who he is to you. I got the impression last night that he was a disrespectful hater, and that's the impression I'm always gonna have of him. But he's your husband, something that you knew but failed to tell me when we first met. I know there's a reason why you didn't wanna tell me, and you can tell me the reason if you want."

"Because I am lonely like how you asked me, okay? I just want another friend."

"I don't have any female friends," he informed her. "I love women, so I always like for them to be more than friends and available to me whenever I wanna see them. Now that I'm getting divorced, I can do whatever the fuck I want and not have to worry about that bitch-ass, soon-to-be ex-wife of mine always on my back and always trying to be up in my social media pages and in my DMs and calling and texting me all the time and shit. I don't need that shit. *I* run everything, not her, that's why we're getting a divorce. She overstepped her role way too much. I warned her but she kept doing it. *I'm* the boss of everything, not her. I'm never getting married again when we're officially divorced. I'm already living my life as if I'm a single man and I'm loving every second of it."

She was practically speechless. "But . . . what am I to you since you say you don't have female friends and I'm married?"

A mischievous smile lit up his face. "Anything I want you to be."

Lisa shook her head as she wrote an entry in her diary after dinner later on that night:

My goodness, I honestly don't know if *I* even wanna talk to Nigel anymore. He's the ultimate alpha male; the boss, the king of every fuckin' thing. He knows he has the power and exercises it to the fullest. I thought we were friends, but he told me he has no female friends, so it wasn't hard for me to really figure out what he uses women for and had done it throughout his marriage to Aisha, who, by the way, he totally disrespected. The mother of his children, a woman he'd been with since high school, people have said. I can't believe the way he was talking about her like that. Greg has *never, ever* in our 10 years of marriage and ever since the day we've known each other, *never, ever* disrespected me like that.

Why would any woman want a serious relationship with him when he is officially divorced? He even said he wants women to be "anything he wants her to be"—that's *crazy*!

Greg said last night he didn't want me talking to him anymore, and he has no idea about me seeing him, and I went against what he said. But if I didn't go against it, I would've never seen for myself what Greg was really talking about, and sometimes we need to see things for ourselves about how people really are so we can form our own opinions about them. And my opinion about Nigel is that I feel he still has a good side to him, and hopefully he will find a woman who can bring that out in him so he can show it all the time instead of only showing it when he wants to.

CHAPTER SEVEN

"Thanks for coming over here today, man. I know you have the day off so I really appreciate it," Greg said to his best friend Mitchell, as he sat at his desk in his office at work.

"No problem, man. You know I'm gonna come here and see what's up with what's been going on with you and Lisa since she met Nigel Foreman. I'm your best friend, man, so I always got the time to talk to you."

"Thank you, man; appreciate it," Greg said once again, and then sighed and shook his head. "I think she's seeing him in person, man, even though she hasn't said anything about seeing him. She told me she was at Starbucks earlier, but I just can't get myself to believe her. Nigel is the type of man who can get any woman he wants, but he's not getting mine."

"I don't blame you, man, for that. I loved what you did at the restaurant that night. He tried to clown you and he got clowned right back. That's the way to do it, man!"

They slapped hands.

"And I didn't even hesitate about doing it, either. I know what he was trying to do and I told her I didn't want her speaking to him again."

"I hope she listens to you, man, because Nigel's a damn trip. He's fucked up on so many levels, man. You know since I'm a civil engineer I know people who used to work for his construction company and they said he was the worst boss ever. He knows how to make money, but it's unbelievable how he can make so much money but not be able to keep people because he acts so nasty towards the people who work for him. I knew from the start when I got into my career that I was not gonna wanna work for him or for anyone in his family."

"I don't blame you, man. He's not only into construction, but I know his family has restaurants, clothing stores, a lot other stuff as well. It's like they're a modern-day Black Wall Street."

"Can't argue with that, man. And you know why all of those women are after him and have always been after him even though he was married to Aisha for fifteen years. It meant nothing to him. My wife was talking about the women where she works at talking about trying to get with him and everything, including ones that are married, single moms, you name it."

Greg shook his head. "Damn shame. They know damn well they shouldn't even entertain the thought."

Mitchell kept staring at him in curiosity. "Um, Lisa is not trying to get with him, is she? You know, even though he came up to her that day?"

"She better not be, man, or she's gonna see a side of me that she's never seen before," he warned.

"Now don't go doing anything crazy, man. I know Lisa, but you know her way better than I do. She's a beautiful, classy woman. I see why Nigel came up to her at that shop that day. Hell, if I didn't know her and didn't know she was married and I wasn't married myself I would've came up to her as well."

He smiled. "I know, man. But Lisa's a grown woman so she's old enough to know better. It's just that if she has seen him since meeting him—and I'm not talking about when he showed up at the restaurant on our date night—then she better tell me. She doesn't know it, but if I think she's lying to me and I have a feeling that she is, I'm gonna have to consider hiring a private investigator."

Mitchell threw his hands up in the air. "Hey, do what you gotta do, man. Y'all been married for ten years and you've never had to do anything like this before. Nigel is toxic. He knows he has the money and everything a woman would want to be with him. He doesn't give a shit if she's married or not."

"Well, he better mess with someone else's wife because mine is off limits and will always be off limits, and I'm putting out a warning to him and her. Like I said, I don't wanna have to show a side of me that she's never seen before, but if I have to then I'm gonna have to do what I gotta do, and he's especially not gonna like it."

CHAPTER EIGHT

"Where's your husband?" Nigel asked Lisa as they sat once again in his recreation room watching TV. She felt she'd never left there.

"He had a late meeting all of the sudden, so when that happens I usually have to eat what I cooked for the both of us, but it—"

"Definitely always means you're on your own for the night—right?"

She smiled. "Yeah, that's right."

He continued to stare at her. "You sure are beautiful, Lisa."

"Thank you," she said as she blushed.

"I don't think your husband realizes what he's got."

She sighed. "Sometimes I don't think he does, either. I know he works hard and I always appreciate how he built a great life for us since we got married and worked on it even before we did, but sometimes I just feel so lonely and bored. It's like he doesn't want me to have friends—*male* friends."

"Can't blame him for that, actually. Like I said, I don't have female friends. I just enjoy a woman's company. I feel that being friends just ruins that; doesn't feel right to me."

"That's understandable," she replied with a smile. "But I know you'll end up with another girlfriend."

"Yeah, I will, but not another wife," he declared.

She chuckled. "I understand. Marriage definitely isn't for everyone, and sometimes you have to find out when you're actually married to see that it isn't for you."

"And I hung in there for fifteen years, but I knew when enough was enough, and she knew it was coming as well so that's why she never tried to fight me about it and we agreed mutually to call it quits."

"Well, that's good since it was on a mutual basis."

His eyes continued to scan her from head to toe. "It is."

She started to feel uncomfortable as she shifted in her seat. "So, what do you look for in a woman?"

"Someone like you," he replied with a smile.

She blushed once again. "Wow, I'm flattered, Nigel. Considering the fact that you can have any woman you want you say someone like me."

"I never lie when it comes to what I want," he informed her. "Too bad you're not available."

"Yeah, I'm not. Sorry."

"No problem," he replied as he still stared her down. "Do you have any tattoos?"

"No, I don't," she informed him. "Greg hates them on women, and I'm scared as hell of needles."

"Now that's something that the two of us have in common. I hate them as well on women, but as you see I have several of them." He sat back in his chair. "Show me."

"Show you?" she asked in total confusion. "Show you what?"

"Show me that you don't have any tattoos," he replied as gave her a sexy grin.

"Are you serious, Nigel?"

"Does it look like I'm kidding?" he asked. "I wanna see that you have no tattoos. They're a turn-off for me. If you don't have any then I want you to prove it to me."

She sat stiff in her seat. She grabbed her bottle of water and took a very hard swallow. She knew she was stuck between a rock and a hard place and knew exactly where his mind was at this moment.

"You . . . mean you want me to . . . *strip*?" she asked in a nervous tone.

"From your head to your toes," he informed her. He stood up. "Do it now. I wanna see that you're not lying to me."

A nervous chill rippled through her body. She got up while he sat back down and watched her.

"There's no one here, is there?"

"Now why would anyone be here? I live here alone. I told you that when I first met you."

"Yeah, you did," she said, as she still stood in the same spot.

"What are you waiting for?" he asked as he glared at her.

She sighed. "I . . ."

"Do it," he demanded.

She still stood in the same spot, unsure of what to do. She felt that he'd felt they'd seen each other enough where he wanted to start getting physical, and this was his way of it leading to his unwavering desires.

She tried to control her breathing as she slowly unbuttoned her jeans and slid them off. She looked up at him.

He nodded. "Turn around."

She turned completely around for him, showing him that she had no tattoos on her legs.

"Beautiful legs," he replied as he still stared at her. "Go on."

"What?"

"Go on, I said. I wanna see the rest of you."

She knew she'd gotten herself into something she knew she couldn't get out of. No man had ever even seen her with just her underwear on except Greg . . . but she still had her top, bra, and panties on, and she wanted to do whatever she could to keep them on.

"Nigel, I don't have any tattoos anywhere. My legs not having any tattoos is how the rest of my body looks."

"I'll believe it when I see it," he replied. "Go on."

She felt tears welling up in her eyes as she took her top off. He smiled as he nodded in approval. "Can I put my top and jeans back on?"

"Not until I see the rest of you," he replied as he sat back in his chair as the left side of his face was held up by his index finger and thumb. "Turn around."

Now just in her bra and panties, she turned around for him. He nodded once again in approval.

"Take the rest off."

She stood stiff as she stared at him.

"It's okay. It's just us here. I'm not gonna tell anyone about this. It's none of anyone's business."

She nodded . . . and slowly removed her bra, and then panties.

"Yeah, this is what I'm talking about right here!" he said. "Damn, you got my dick all motherfuckin' hard, baby, shit!" he said. "You weren't lying. You don't have any tattoos on you. You've got a beautiful body."

"Thank you," she replied in a soft tone, but never felt so uncomfortable. She'd never done anything like this ever before and knew she could never forgive herself. "Can I put my clothes back on?"

"Not yet," he replied, and got out of his chair and stood right in front her. "Damn, you're so beautiful, Lisa. So real, so natural. I love it."

"Thank you," she said once again, and felt herself getting very moist *down there* with him standing so close to her.

He embraced her. "You don't have to be afraid of me, okay? I'm here to make you feel good; to make you feel wanted. You don't ever have to worry about feeling lonely with me." He took off his jeans, underwear, and sat back down in his seat. "Jerk me off."

She'd never stood so stunned before in her life. "What?!"

"You heard me, Lisa. Jerk me off. I love it when a woman does it to me. Don't tell me you've never jerked off a man before."

"Yeah, I have," she said with a little embarrassment.

He chuckled. "That's what I thought. Come here, baby. I wanna see one or both of those pretty hands of yours wrapped around my hard-ass dick right now."

"I . . . I can't, Nigel," she said, and looked at her watch. "I gotta go. I know Greg is gonna be home soon."

"You can go after you jerk me off," he informed her. "The sooner you get over here and do it and I cum fast, the sooner you can leave."

She slowly walked over to him as he smiled at her. She got in front of him and bent down. She breathed heavy as she wrapped both of her hands around his dick and started moving it up and down in fast strokes as he breathed heavy while moaning louder and louder until his satisfaction echoed all throughout the room and physically showed.

He continued to breathe heavy as he opened his eyes. "Damn, that was good. I needed that. Thank you, Mrs. Everett."

"You're welcome," she squeaked out.

She turned the lights on in the kitchen . . . .

"Where were you?" Greg asked, as he sat at the kitchen island counter.

"Over at Chassy's," she lied.

"No you weren't because I called her and she told me you weren't there." He got up out of his seat and stood in front of her. She was scared stiff. "You have one more chance to tell me where you were, Lisa, I'm serious. And the answer better not be Sharita's because I know you weren't there as well because I called her and she said you weren't there."

She let out a long, loud sigh. "I was just out driving around, okay? I just have to get out of the house. You said at the last minute that you had a meeting so I didn't have to cook after all so I just went to get something to eat and ate in the fast-food restaurant parking lot, and then just sat there for a while looking at my phone and then came home."

"Give me the receipt from your food," he demanded.

"I didn't get it. They asked me if I wanted it and I said I didn't because I didn't need it," she replied.

He continued to glare at her, unsure if he wanted to believe a word she'd said. "If you're seeing Nigel, Lisa, you better tell me right now, and I mean *right now*!"

"Are you seeing someone?" she asked.

"What? Where the fuck did that shit come from? You know damn well I'm not seeing anyone behind your back, Lisa. You know it. Since we've been together I've never cheated on you, *never*, so you better not be doing it to me, I mean it."

"I'm not, Greg! I said where I was, okay? And I'm not gonna say it again. If you don't believe me then fine, there's nothing I can do about it. I'm tired. I'm gonna get to bed early." She walked away from him while he still stood in the kitchen while shaking his head.

Several minutes later, she walked out into the hall and heard Greg in his den talking on the phone while the cheers and jeers from a game blasted on his TV. She walked back into their bedroom and took her computer out and wrote in her diary:

Greg is on to me. He knows that I've been seeing Nigel even though he can't prove it. I went way too far with him tonight. He wanted to see if I had any tattoos and made me take off all of my clothes to prove I didn't and yes, I did it. I feel so bad, so ashamed. I've never done anything like that for another man while being married. I felt I betrayed Greg's trust. I broke our wedding vows. Once again, I didn't have intercourse with Nigel, but another man saw me naked other than my husband, so yes, I feel like I cheated on him because I did.

But I can't help to say that there's something about Nigel that makes me feel so good to be in his presence. I know I shouldn't say this, but I can't help but to think it. He has a way of making a woman feel that he only wants to be with her, even though the whole world knows that's not true. Sometimes I just don't know what to do. Seeing him takes me away from all of the problems I have right now with Greg and everyone and everything else. Oh, and Greg told me he wasn't cheating on me when he asked me was I cheating on him. I know I shouldn't have answered a question with a question but I had to know, but I have no way of knowing for sure if he's actually telling me the truth. But I know something that is for sure, I don't want to stop seeing Nigel . . . .

Even after jerking him off. Like I said, we didn't have intercourse—I just can't do it—but just doing what I did to him and showing him my naked body was cheating on Greg, and I've never cheated on him before. I feel so bad making for Nigel feel so good, but I just can't stop seeing him. Being confused is an understatement.

What the hell is wrong with me?

Several hours later, she woke up out of a deep sleep. She looked to her left and Greg was not in bed with her. She got up out of bed and walked around the house to look for him. She found him downstairs sleeping on the couch, something he hadn't done in the ten years they'd been married.

CHAPTER NINE

It was the second Sunday of the month, and this meant the family and friends of Lisa's side of the family as well as family and friends of her in-laws, met at her parents' house for the Sunday Soul Feast, which had all of the mouth-watering soul food everyone loved . . . except chitlins.

Mother Martha—as Lisa's mom was called—did most of the cooking, but had a team of qualified cooks help her for this once-a-month get-together. No one was allowed in her kitchen who didn't know how to cook or thought they could cook. Only the best would do because Mother Martha claimed she was the best soul food cook in the world, but had no plans on opening her own restaurant.

As usual, everyone was here and enjoyed the bright and sunny afternoon, and most stayed until late in the evening or when they'd clearly worn out their welcome.

Lisa and Sharita sat in a corner away from most people as they held a conversation they didn't want anyone else to hear.

"So, you *bared it all* for Nigel, huh? *And* jerked him off? Lisa, what the hell has gotten into you?" Sharita asked in a whisper, and then took a sip of her soda.

"That's a good question, Sharita. I really can't answer that for you. I know what I did was wrong and like I wrote in my diary, Greg is on to me. We haven't talked like we usually do for a few days now, and even came here in separate cars."

"You did?!" she asked in a very surprised tone. "Wow, Lisa. I didn't know things were getting this bad between the two of you."

"Well, I don't wanna say things are getting *that* bad, it's just that we are having problems like any couple will have and I know it's getting to him a lot that we still can't have children, but when you look around here, you wouldn't think anyone had a problem," Lisa replied, as she watched young kids running around carefree and even some women and men holding newborn babies or ones that were only a few months old.

"Well, just because everyone here seems to have kids doesn't mean that they're a hundred percent happy, Lisa. I can attest to that myself."

She sighed. "It's just that when I see Nigel, I feel like I'm in a whole other world, you know?"

"That's because he *is* in a whole other world, Lisa. The man is the one percent of the one percent as they say. You won't see him at get-togethers like this. They probably have theirs in a palace that they own or something. His life is a lot different than ours."

"And I admit I always wondered what that would be like, you know?"

"Yeah, I know. I think we all do who don't live like that. But what's so wrong with the way you're living now? You live better than anyone here."

"Sometimes I feel that it's just not enough, and I'm not talking about materialism, you know? I'm bored, I'm lonely, and I admit that Nigel gives me some kind of weird excitement—it's something that's hard to explain, but at the same time, I get so nervous around him because I know that it's wrong for me to keep seeing him the way I am. I know I'll never seriously be with him or anyone like him since I'm married, but I do wonder what it would be like."

"Just be happy with who you're with, Lisa. You and Greg may be having problems right now, but there isn't any problem the two of you can't get through."

Lisa looked over at Greg who sat with a group of men while they played cards. They locked eyes. He looked away and focused his attention back on the men playing cards even though he wasn't playing with them. She sighed. "I just don't know if I'm that happy anymore."

A man jumped up out of his seat as if it was on fire!

"Hey, everyone! I just got something on my phone that's saying one of Nigel Foreman's baby mamas was found dead! DAMN!"

Some people gasped, some didn't, but all of them looked at their phones and saw the same information popping up on theirs as well.

"Holy shit!" Sharita said as she looked at Lisa . . . and she wasn't the only one.

Lisa scanned the area and saw most looking at her since a lot of people she knew that she'd met him, but none knew what Sharita had known and what Greg had suspected. She locked eyes with Greg once again. He glared at her, put back on his sunglasses, and looked at his phone.

"What is going on with the two of you, Lisa? Everyone noticed that the two of you came in separate cars and didn't speak to each other the entire time you were here," Mother Martha asked her while they sat inside in the kitchen eating banana pudding and drinking coffee after everyone had left for the day. The roaring of her dad's snoring could be heard in the family room.

"He's still upset that I haven't gotten pregnant yet," she replied, as she picked at her pudding with her fork.

"That's understandable. We all are, baby, but it's gonna happen for the two of you. It just seems like something else is wrong."

"There is," she admitted.

"And what is it?"

"He thinks I'm cheating on him. And not only cheating on him, he thinks I'm cheating on him with—"

"Nigel Foreman?" she asked.

"How did you know?"

"You know Momma, girl. I hear about things you act like you don't wanna tell me about. So, are you?"

"No, Momma, I'm not," she lied.

She gave her a look of skepticism.

"I'm not, and I didn't appreciate everyone looking at me today as if I am. I don't know what the hell Greg has been telling people, but I'm gonna have to have a serious talk with him when I get home because I do wanna know if he's telling people that I am."

"Honey, I don't think he is. You know he's not that kind of person. But I think he is suspecting something so it's up to you to set him straight about everything. I hope you're telling the truth, Lisa. You know I raised you to have respect for yourself and to get a decent man and get married to him—and you did that. But I also told you once you got that decent man to not cheat on him with another man, I don't care how much he has. That Nigel I know can give a woman the world, but there's a reason why he's getting a divorce. And what is all this about *one* of his baby mamas being found dead?"

"Yeah, while he was married he fathered four kids out of wedlock by three different women, now one of them is dead."

"Oh, good Lord! What a mess! Do you know anything about it?"

"No, Momma, not a thing. I'm serious. I may have talked to Nigel, but he didn't tell me anything about any of his baby mamas. All three of them were pretty much outspoken on social media and everything, so maybe the one who was killed said something she shouldn't have."

"How do you know she was killed and not just found dead of some other cause?"

"Momma, I really don't know. I'm just assuming she was killed because it definitely could be foul play. I really don't know, like I said, and I *don't* wanna get involved."

"Okay, you better not. Don't let that man try and make you believe he had nothing to do with it when he probably did."

"Please don't say that, Momma."

"Well, I'm just being real, Lisa. It's best that you don't talk to him anymore, especially now. You got your husband and a family to start and we're all excited and praying for the two of you. You live better than most people. You don't need anyone like Nigel Foreman who's getting a divorce and may now have a pending murder charge on him."

"Momma!"

"Just remember what I said, honey. *Please.*"

"Greg?" Lisa said as she walked into his den. "We need to talk."

He sighed as he glared at her. "About what, Lisa? About how your lover was questioned in the murder of one of his baby mamas? Do you know anything about it?"

"No, I don't know a damn thing about it, Greg. That's the first thing I want you to know. Second of all, Nigel and I are *not* lovers, so stop saying that. I also want you to know that I thought it was very rude and nasty of you to act as if you didn't wanna talk to me the whole time we were at my parents' house today. You embarrassed me as well as yourself acting like that. Everyone noticed that we came in separate cars and acted as if we didn't know each other, and my mom asked me about it when everyone left."

"I don't care what people think, Lisa. You know why I didn't wanna talk to you; you know why we haven't been sleeping together."

"Because you think I'm sleeping with Nigel?"

He continued to glare at her. "Are you?"

"No, Greg, I'm not! I wish you would stop thinking that! You think just because he's this mega-rich black man that I'm fucking him? I'm *not!*"

"But you're still talking to him, aren't you?"

She lowered her head.

He shook his head as he let out a sarcastic laugh. "Yeah, that's what I thought." He gave her a piercing glare. "You just *can't* leave a man like that alone, can you? What is it that I have to do to make you stop talking to him?"

"Nothing, Greg. I just don't see any harm in it. I mean, I won't get mad if there's a woman you always talked to that you just liked talking to as a friend."

"Bullshit."

She let out a sigh. "Can we just stop this, please? It's wearing me out. You wanna know why I probably haven't gotten pregnant yet? Well, it's probably because of stress and I'm tired of being stressed out!" she said as tears welled up in her eyes.

He got up out of his seat. "Hey, baby. I'm sorry, okay? You know I never mean to stress you out. But you have to learn how to deal with everyday stress because we all have it. Look, I'll make a deal with you. I'll stop asking you about Nigel, okay? Because it looks like at this point he's in enough trouble, and I have to admit that I'm curious to know if he murdered her, but I know you had nothing to do with knowing anything about it. So, no more talk about you and Nigel, deal?"

She smiled as tears continued to stream down her eyes. "Deal."

"Come on, let me make you some of your favorite tea and we can watch one of those old black movies from the 30s and 40s that you love."

"Sounds great, honey. You know I have a preference for Oscar Micheaux films."

"Naturally."

They walked with their arms around each other downstairs to the kitchen, but she knew she couldn't stop speaking to Nigel now. She had to find out everything she could about what'd happened to one of his baby mamas and why. She went to the bathroom while Greg made her tea. She looked at her phone . . .

It was Nigel.

CHAPTER TEN

"Do you have any idea who could've killed her?" Lisa asked Nigel the next day as she sat with him in his kitchen while they ate lunch since he had a few days off because of what'd happened to one of his baby mamas, and it was confirmed that it was a homicide.

"No, I have no idea, Lisa. All I know is that it wasn't me so that's why I went to the police with my lawyer to clear my name. He suggested that I do it because he said I was gonna be questioned regardless because she's the mother of one of my kids," he said, and then took a sip of his soda.

"Wow, I just can't believe this happened to one of them. It's really tragic and sad. Everyone's talking about it and saying all sorts of stuff like—"

He slammed his fork down on the table!

She shrieked in shock!

"I don't give a fuck what people are saying, Lisa, okay? All I wanna know is who did this to her because I sure as hell didn't. I don't wanna hear anything but the truth. Now one of my kids doesn't have their mom."

"But your child still has you."

"Yeah, whatever. But she can't live with me because I'm too busy and I'm not going through hiring nannies and all sorts of people to take care of one child. She's already been sent to live with her mom's parents. I feel that it's the best arrangement since they are her biological grandparents. My parents said she couldn't live with them since they rarely acknowledge her or my other three kids who were born out of wedlock even though they accepted that the kids are their grandkids. I know this is my fault and I fucked up and I've lived with the consequences of it. If there's anything no one can say it's that I haven't been taking care of them financially."

She smiled. "Well, that's good. You have more than enough money to do that."

"Yeah, I'll always have money, but that doesn't mean I want more kids. I'm done with that shit like I'm done with Aisha and being married. Period."

"I understand. Some things just don't work out. Well, I hope we all find out who killed Taylor for the sake of her family and especially y'alls daughter."

"Yeah, I hope so, too. But I know I didn't do it so I'm not worried about being questioned again. As far as I'm concerned, my name is completely off the suspects' list."

She didn't wanna say anything to make him mad as she had minutes before, but she couldn't help but to think that something nefarious could've been going on when it came to him and his involvement with what'd happened to Taylor. She knew this was very hard for him to deal with and didn't wanna complicate any matters. She stayed silent for the rest of the time as they ate their lunch because deep down inside, she just couldn't a hundred percent rule him out.

She shook her head as she wrote in her diary hours later:

I just talked to Nigel for the first time since one of his baby mamas was murdered. It was his first baby mama, Taylor. She has one child by him. That poor little girl; now she doesn't have a mother and has a dad who doesn't want her living with him. Yes, I did say murdered because that's what her cause of death is ruled as, he told me, and it was confirmed by several news reports. I just feel so uneasy talking to him. He called me last night right before Greg and I watched a movie—yes, we made up—but I ignored the call because of Greg. But when he called me again in the morning, I felt I had to see him and talk about this because I felt that he needed someone to talk to. We had lunch at his house since he didn't wanna go anywhere and took a few days off from work because of what'd happened, and he told me he talked to the police yesterday with his lawyer present and said he cleared his name . . . .

But have the police officially cleared him?

Is he really off of their suspects' list like he told me he is?

I thought he was gonna stab me with the fork he slammed down on the table when all I said was something about people saying all sorts of stuff about the case which is true— it obviously set off something in him, like he knew something that he didn't wanna tell me. But what he also told me and made it very clear was that he didn't want any more kids and said that their daughter is gonna live with her grandparents because his parents want nothing to do with her because she was born out of wedlock. I think that's very sad and very mean and disrespectful of his parents to act that way towards a child who didn't ask to be born under the circumstances to which she was born under—but that's the way a lot of people are.

Nigel has gotten himself in a big mess, and I just feel that things will eventually get better for him, and I say that because he's being positive about things which is what he needs to be. But I can say I definitely saw that other side of him come out, and I honestly don't wanna see it again. And because I saw that side of him, I just can't say that he's a hundred percent innocent in all of this.

Lisa and Greg laid in bed later that night when the news began with Breaking News in regard to the murder of Taylor:

"We have Breaking News this evening. Aisha Foreman, estranged wife of the High-Nine-Figure Man Nigel Foreman, breaks her silence in the murder of one his children's mothers, Taylor Drummond."

The news went to the clip which showed Aisha Foreman as she stood between her lawyers dressed head to toe in a Giorgio Armani black Ottoman bustier-style jacket with black pants and shoes, Tom Ford black sunglasses, and a black Hermes Birkin 35 Epsom leather bag with palladium hardware resting in the crook of her arm.

"Damn, she's gotten *fat*! No wonder why Nigel's divorcing her," Greg said with a huge grin.

"Greg! That's not nice! And if that is one of the reasons then that's sad, and I hope that's not the main reason because I know there are other reasons, there has to be."

He looked at her. "Yeah, I just bet you do know there are other reasons, Lisa."

"Greg, don't start. I thought we weren't gonna do this anymore."

"Well, we won't have to do this anymore if you did what I

wanted you to do in terms of not speaking to him anymore much less seeing him, especially now since he's in this mess and I feel that he had something to do with it, and I don't care how much he tries to convince everyone otherwise. And he better not even think about trying to drag you into all of his mess as well."

"Greg, he's not gonna drag me into anything, okay? A lot of people are always gonna think he had something to do with it since Taylor was one of his baby mamas. Let's hear what Aisha has to say."

He nodded as he stared at her, and then focused his attention back to the TV.

"I'm Aisha Foreman. I'm the soon-to-be ex-wife of Nigel Foreman. I would like to first extend my deepest condolences to the family of Taylor Drummond. No matter how much Nigel had his indiscretions all throughout our fifteen-year marriage, I never wanted this to happen to one of the mothers of his children. I have fully cooperated with the authorities regarding this matter and I will continue to cooperate with them. I just wanna say on record that I had nothing to do with this, absolutely nothing. Please pray for Nigel's daughter and that her mother's killer will be caught and justice will be rightfully served. Thank you."

Aisha walked off with her lawyers as a swarm of media followed them and got into an awaiting black Bentley Mulsanne.

Greg looked at Lisa. "Do you believe her?"

"Yeah, I actually do. I don't think Aisha was that mad that she killed one of Nigel's baby mamas. If that were the case then she would've did it or had someone do it when she first found out that Taylor had a baby by her husband."

"That's true, but maybe Nigel left her for Taylor since she was his first baby mama. Man, that motherfucker is a damn hot mess!"

"I honestly don't know, Greg. Nigel told me he wanted out of the marriage for a while and that's all I know because you told me not to talk to him anymore so I'm doing just that," she lied.

He stared at her, unsure if he should've believed her. "You better, Lisa. I mean it. Even though I'm interested in what's going on in this case because I know it concerns him a great deal, it doesn't mean that I want you talking to him. I still stand by everything I said and there's no way I'm changing my mind."

She sighed. "Greg, I know." *But until I find out who killed Taylor, I just can't stop talking to him, much less seeing him. He needs me because if he didn't then why did he call me about wanting to talk about this? He could've called anyone, but he called me. Me,* she thought.

CHAPTER ELEVEN

"Look, Chassy, there's something I need to tell you," Lisa said, while she sat in the family room of Chassy's home since she had the day off work.

Chassy's eyes got big. "What is it, Lisa? You know you can tell me anything, girl. Just say it."

Lisa shook her head. "I just don't know how to say it." She stared at her. "Please don't get mad when I tell you—"

"That you met Nigel Foreman that day in the shop when I was in bathroom?" she asked with a grin, but glared at her at the same time.

Lisa looked shocked. "What? How did you know, Chassy?"

"I knew for a while, Lisa. I was just waiting for you to tell me, that's all. I have to admit I was mad at first, but I meant everything I said when I said I have no chance with a man like Nigel."

"No woman has a serious chance with Nigel anymore since he told me he's never getting married again. He said Aisha was enough for him."

She smiled. "Yeah, I can believe that. He didn't seem fully happy when he was married for those fifteen years, but he didn't have to father four kids out of wedlock because of it, now his first baby mama is dead, but not only dead, murdered. Damn! That's really fucked up when you think about it, you know?"

"Yeah, I know."

"So, how much have you talked to him?"

"Just about every day. And no, Greg does not like the fact that I talk to him."

"Well, you can't blame him for that, Lisa. Greg's your husband, not Nigel."

"I know that. But when I talk to Nigel, I just feel like I'm in another world; a better world."

"I honestly don't see what you see so wrong about the world you live in now. Most women will kill to be in your position, Lisa, including me."

"Would they love the fact that I can't seem to get pregnant? Who would want to deal with that? Plus, boredom and loneliness because I live a life where I don't have to work because Greg wants it this way so he built this life for us this way. It gets boring after a while when it seems like I've done everything many times over."

"Well, I'll trade places with you any day. Just because I'm back with my second baby daddy doesn't mean I can afford the kind of luxuries that you have always been able to afford. I still have to work and take care of my four kids, and he still acts as if he doesn't wanna move in when I offered, so I just don't know how this is all gonna work out after all."

"Just stay positive, Chassy. It's clear he likes having his own space."

"True, and I am staying positive. But you honestly need to stop talking to Nigel, Lisa. I was jealous of the fact that he came up to you —I saw that woman's selfie on social media with him standing by our table talking to you—that's how I found out, but I was waiting for you to tell me."

"Sorry," she replied.

"It's okay, Lisa. It's clear that he was far more attracted to you than he would be to me and I accepted that because it was not surprising at all. But now that you do know him, I'm gonna join in with Greg and say that I don't want you talking to him or seeing him as well. I don't think he's been a hundred percent ruled out in Taylor's murder, so don't think for a second that he has been."

"I know, Chassy, I'm not naïve in the fact that someone can talk and talk and talk to your face about being innocent when they're anything but that. It's just that I find Nigel intriguing in a weird way. I guess talking to him takes me away from the problems I'm having with Greg and everyone else just always meddling in our business; my business. Nigel told me he didn't have female friends, so I don't know what I should consider our relationship to be."

"You shouldn't have any kind of relationship with him, Lisa, I'm serious. It's just something about him now since you've met him and one of his baby mamas was murdered. I would just stay away from him and continue to focus on your marriage to Greg and starting y'alls family. Greg's wealth may not match Nigel's, and that's okay. Greg, to me, is just a better person. I heard Nigel wasn't that nice after all."

"To be honest, he's not. When I was over his house yesterday to talk about Taylor's murder—and please don't tell Greg I was over there."

"I won't," she pledged.

"Well, when I just simply told him that a lot of people are really talking on social media about the case and who could've done it, he slammed his fork down so hard I thought he broke it—and we were eating with some very expensive silverware—he scared the shit out of me. He said he didn't care what people were saying and even told me his daughter by Taylor was not gonna be living with him but with her grandparents on her mom's side because his parents wanted nothing to do with caring for her since she was born out of wedlock."

"That is so wrong. Being born out of wedlock or not, that's still their grandchild, like it or not. Damn, Lisa. Sounds to me like his whole family is fucked up. It just shows you that money can't buy decency and goodwill. It amazes me how wealthy they all are because of the way they act. The only one who seems decent is Aisha, and I know she's glad she won't be with Nigel anymore."

"Yeah, she seems to be a genuinely nice woman when she was on the news giving a statement to the media about the case. She seems like she was a great woman for him, but it's unfortunate he didn't feel the same way about her, and I know he didn't because he constantly talked shit about her to me when I was over his house before yesterday."

She shook her head. "Now I'll admit I was caught up with his looks and money and everything, but that shit doesn't matter to me anymore at all, and it shouldn't matter to any woman and it especially shouldn't matter to you. You need to stop talking to him and especially seeing him every time he contacts you, Lisa. Change your contact info; go private on your social media pages since he doesn't follow you anyway, you said. It sounds to me that he just uses women for his own benefit, and when he gets tired of her, he'll just throw her in a trash bin and be on to the next. Did he even show any kind of concern or sadness about what'd happened to Taylor?"

She didn't even think about this while she'd talked to him. "No, I have to admit that he didn't. He didn't shed one tear. I wasn't even thinking about it at the time but now you made me think back. No, he really didn't. Wow, it's like he really doesn't care."

"That's because he doesn't. He's probably happy that Taylor was murdered so he doesn't have to deal with her anymore even though their child is still here. He's bad news, Lisa. I now see him in a whole other light and it's not a good one. Stop talking to him and especially seeing him like I said. Listen to Greg as well."

"And my mom. She said the same thing at the Sunday get-together this month."

"Yeah, and if she said it then you really need to listen, Lisa. We all love you and care about you, and don't wanna see you get hurt by a guy like Nigel. He thinks just because of his wealth and power and privilege that he can do whatever he wants. Please don't let a man like that manipulate you into doing shit for him where it only bene-fits him."

"What do you mean?"

"I mean anything. I know you don't know him that well, but what you've told me just doesn't sound good. It doesn't sit right with me. Greg is a great man. Count your blessings in that aspect and please leave men like Nigel alone."

Lisa wrote in her diary after her talk with Chassy:

Wow, even Chassy wants me to leave Nigel alone, and I can't say I blame her; can't blame anyone. Got done talking to her over an hour ago. But they don't talk to Nigel like the way I have. He's not all that bad as he seems or what I made him out to be. He definitely has his bad side, but who doesn't? And I just can't get myself to believe that he had something to do with Taylor's murder, but then on the other hand, I can't a hundred percent rule him out since it's always in the back of my mind about the possibility because anything's possible.

I'm confused as I can be right now. I honestly don't know what to think about anything anymore. Maybe I can keep talking to him until he admits something incriminating about Taylor's murder so I can at least do the right thing and go to the cops with it—but then again, what am I talking about? I'm not a detective. I have to admit that I am making excuses to still wanna talk to him because despite what everyone is saying to me, I just still feel there is no harm in it. We haven't had sex or anything and he hasn't hurt me in any way, so as long as that doesn't happen then I'm fine and there's nothing wrong with continuing on with seeing him, but it's definitely gonna have to be our little secret.

CHAPTER TWELVE

"So, what is up with you and that woman Lisa, man? I thought you weren't seeing her anymore?" Nigel's best friend, Jerry, asked.

"Nothing is up with her; she's married. We just like talking and seeing each other, at least she likes seeing me," Nigel said, as they sat in his recreation room watching TV.

"So you don't like seeing her?"

"She's okay, man. She's just another woman I talk to, that's all. I'm getting divorced so it doesn't matter who I talk to now. Aisha can't say shit. Everything is all out in the open."

"Well, with your three baby mamas, man, was anything ever in secret?"

Nigel grinned. "No, I guess I can say that it wasn't!"

They laughed.

"But it is fucked up what happened to Taylor, though," Jerry said as he shook his head, and then took a swig out of his glass of hard liquor.

"Yeah, it is, but I had nothing to do with it and I told Lisa that because I know for some reason she thinks I did have something to do with it. I just need to set her straight about everything. She just asks a lot of questions that I feel she shouldn't be asking."

"Why, man?"

"Because it's none of her business, that's why. I don't know why any of what I do or what happens in my life concerns her. But she's one of those married, bored, nosey, lonely women who just wants to talk since her husband works all the time and they have no kids."

"Her husband was out of line for doing that shit to you at the restaurant, man."

"Well, he's a hater and I told her he was a hater. A very disrespectful hater. She just kept saying how sorry she was to me for what he did and was constantly saying he was a nice guy—blah, blah, blah. I didn't give a shit about any of that or him. It's clear that she constantly wants to see me since she's always calling and texting me," Nigel said, as he tried to make him believe that she was the one getting obsessed with him.

"Do you want her to leave you alone?"

"Nah, she's harmless. I'll give her some dick if she wants it; hasn't gotten to that yet with her and I can understand since she's trying to remain a loyal wife to her hating-ass husband, but she showed me she has no tattoos anywhere on her body."

Jerry grinned. "Damn, she stripped completely naked for you, huh? Just like you make all of them do, married or not. Doesn't surprise me, man. She knows she wants to fuck you; she's just trying to be a good little housewife."

"Yeah, she is . . . for now. But she better give me what I want when I want it or I'm gonna have to cut her off for good. I don't need her. I don't need any of these thots out here."

"You sure as hell don't, man. If anything they need you, they'll always need you."

The news broke into the TV show they were watching with Breaking News:

"Sorry for the interruption, but we have Breaking News this

evening. There has been an arrest in the murder of Taylor Drummond, the mother of one of Nigel Foreman's out-of-wedlock children."

"WHAT?!" Nigel and Jerry yelled as they both jumped up out of their chairs at the same time.

They stood in shock as they stared at the TV in complete suspense at what the anchorman was going to say next:

"Police have arrested Ivy Woodard, the second mother of Nigel Foreman's out-of-wedlock children who has two children by the High-Nine-Figure Man. Nigel is known to have four out-of-wedlock children by three different women, with the third being Haniah Knicks, who has a son by him. We haven't been able to reach the Drummond family, nor have we been able to reach the lawyer for Ivy Woodard for comment since we were told she does have a lawyer. Nigel Foreman's lawyers have also been contacted, but no one has returned our calls."

Jerry looked at Nigel.

"And I'm not gonna discuss this until I talk to my lawyers," he replied as he picked up his phone off the chair. "Yeah, I see my lawyers have tried to call me. I'll talk to them soon." He sat back down and let out a huge sigh as he shook his head. "What the fuck would make Ivy do some shit like this? She was getting just as much as Taylor was getting. This shit ain't my fault, man. These bitches are crazy!"

Jerry laughed. "Yeah, they are, man! But this is a big fuckin' hot-ass mess, you have to admit that, at least."

"Never said it wasn't. I just never thought one of my baby mamas would kill the other—and for what? She had no reason to do what she did so she's on her own with this shit. Don't she expect for me to be a character witness or help pay any fees for her defense. I don't want anything to do with this shit. None of it."

Meanwhile, Lisa and Greg were sitting in their family room in complete shock at the news.

"Damn," Greg said as he shook his head. "What the fuck is wrong with these women?"

Lisa shrugged. "I have no idea, Greg. Something obviously happened between the two of them since they both have kids by him."

"*Out-of-wedlock* kids by him, big difference. See, this is the kind of mess my parents wanted me to avoid, and I'm glad I listened to them. I knew you were the right woman when you had the same morals and values that I do."

"You're right, honey. It's too bad Chassy and Sharita and millions of other women are just like Taylor, Ivy, and Haniah."

"But those three are the ultimate thots because they knew Nigel was married and he knew he was married when he fucked them all. The man is a fuckin' hot mess and it wouldn't surprise me if he made that whore kill the other one. Probably promised her more money. What kind of a woman would have not one child by a married man, but two?"

"You'll have to ask her that, Greg."

"No thanks. Keep those thots away from me. They all thought Nigel was gonna leave Aisha and marry them and they see how it didn't happen. He's divorcing, yeah, but you know it's not to be with one of them."

"Yeah, it's not."

He gave her a look of suspicion. "And how do you know that?"

"Well, I don't. I'm just agreeing with you, that's all."

He kept staring at her, unsure if he wanted to believe her or not. "You just remember what I said, Lisa, about not talking to him anymore and especially seeing him. Even though they made an arrest in this case, there is no way I'm ruling him out of anything. A man like that women should not walk from, they need to run from. All he does is cause trouble."

"Yeah, but it wouldn't be trouble if the women didn't have a part in it. They wanted something they thought they were gonna get by having a child, and in Ivy's case, children, by him—that high-nine-figure lifestyle."

"Then they're the stupidest women in the world to think that. I know a toxic man when I see one, and he's it. He doesn't care about anyone but himself. He's probably glad that one of those baby mamas of his is dead and now the other one is gonna be in prison for probably life for it. He practically killed two birds with one stone."

"Don't talk like that, Greg. We know they made an arrest, but we don't know if Ivy did this or not."

"And it's none of our business, Lisa. I'm serious. But you're right. We don't know if Ivy did this or not, and if she didn't, I know who did or if she did, I know who made her do it."

She gasped in shock. "Nigel did *not* make Ivy kill Taylor, Greg! How could you say something like that?"

"How do you know he didn't? Did he tell you?"

She sighed. "It's been said everywhere on his social media pages and all that he had nothing to do with it. He said he had nothing to do with it so why would he lie about that? He has everything in the world going for him and has since the day he was born. There's no way he would mess himself up by doing something so heinous where he even knows it himself that since he's a black man he will get put in jail for life or maybe even get the death penalty."

"Or get acquitted which would more than likely be the case if he did have something to do with it. Money talks, baby, and however this case turns out, I *still* don't want you talking to him or seeing him."

CHAPTER THIRTEEN

"Good afternoon, everyone, I'm Nigel Foreman. I just wanted to say that I am glad that there has been an arrest in the murder of one of my child's mothers, Taylor Drummond. Unfortunately, the connection is too troublesome for me to bring myself to talk about who was arrested in this case, but as you all know she is innocent until proven guilty. My deepest condolences go out to the Drummond family on the loss of their daughter, who was not only a daughter and mother, but also an aunt, cousin, and friend to many. I'm not taking any questions because I have to get back to work, thank you," he said, and walked away under heavy security and the mob of media and flashes from cameras to his awaiting black Bentley Bentayga SUV. He got into the front seat, and the driver drove off from all of the chaos.

"'I have to get back to work, thank you.' Just how in the hell could he think of working at a time like this? Work would be the last thing I would be thinking about if my one of my baby daddies killed the other, but luckily all of my kids are by my boyfriend," Sharita said, and then took a sip of her soda as she and Lisa sat at her house the next day since Sharita coincidentally had the day off from work.

"He has to make a living, Sharita. You know how it is."

She laughed. "Yeah, *I* know how it is, much more than Nigel Foreman will ever know how it is. He's never had any trouble feeding all nine of his kids and he never will. And I know he's responsible for making mostly all of the new money in his family's fortune, but that man could've never worked a day in his life and would *still* live as good as he lives."

"I know that, and he knows that as well. But as you see he's not like that. He's a producer—a *power* producer. That's what I love about him. He may have his flaws, but we all do, and you see how he made a statement about this case. He had nothing to do with it and you can see how he wanted people to know that."

"Oh, yeah? Then how come he didn't flat-out say he had nothing to do with it? Huh? I mean, I hate to say this about him, Lisa, but I can't a hundred percent rule him out of anything. It's just something about it."

She sighed. "I know it seems that way, Sharita, but he told me he had nothing to do with it and I believe him. I don't think he would lie about something this serious, and this is damn serious. One of his children don't have their mother anymore. It's a damn shame that Ivy wanted to be so selfish and take one of the mothers away from her child. She would not have liked it if that happened to her."

"Well, she's a hot mess; they're all a hot mess. But what it all comes down to is that Nigel started this whole hot mess and he knows it. Him speaking today about giving his fake-ass condolences to Taylor's family is something his parents probably made him do, as well as his lawyers. If it was up to him I'm sure he would still be silent about this."

There's only one way to find out, she thought.

CHAPTER FOURTEEN

NIGEL HAD A RARE DINNER WITH ONLY HIS PARENTS, PARKER AND DENISE Foreman, and they said he had no choice in the matter about whether or not he wanted to talk to them since this dinner was mandatory.

His parents—both in their 70s—had aged very well, and it showed on both of them the kind of life they'd lived their whole lives. Since it was Parker's father who started the first business—a bank—that started the Foreman fortune, Parker expanded out into other businesses such as construction, restaurant chains, as well as clothing stores, and as a result, they were responsible for creating their own version of Black Wall Street. And Denise was responsible for raising and eventually grooming Nigel to take over.

But Nigel was Parker and Denise's only child. Through numerous affairs, Parker had fathered many children with several other women outside of his fifty-plus-year marriage to Denise, as his late father had. Nigel was supposed to be the one who broke the cycle and be nothing like his father and grandfather, but he failed miserably and knew it, and they finally wanted to talk to him about it.

"So, son. It looks like you got yourself into a mess you can't get out of," Parker said, as he cut his steak. "What the hell is wrong with all of those women?"

"I don't know, Dad. All I know is that I had nothing to do with it. Ivy did what she did on her own. It's messed up, but hey, I don't know why she would do something like that when like I told everyone, she was getting more money because she has two kids by me and not just one like Taylor and Haniah."

"Did you promise Taylor or Ivy that you were gonna be with them after you and Aisha officially divorce?" Denise asked, and then sipped her champagne.

"Why the hell would I do that, Mom?" Nigel asked in disgust. "I didn't love Aisha. Hate to say this, but I never really did. I only married her because she was pregnant with our first child and because you both and her parents wanted me to. If it was up to me then she would've been like the other three."

Parker laughed. "Yeah, I just know they would've, son. But you know it would've looked bad if you never married her and had all of those children."

"Yeah, you should know," Denise said as she glared at Parker.

"C'mon, Mom and Dad. I didn't come over here to have the two of you get into a fight, okay? I know all about my half brothers and sisters by different women, and you know I'm not close to any of them. I'm glad you put me in charge of everything, Dad. I just don't think any of them can do the job that I can do."

"No, I don't think they can. Some of them have done good with themselves but since they have different mothers, I can't have them in charge of any of the businesses we own. Your grandfather put that in his will and I have to honor it," Parker said.

"Yeah, that's about the only thing you honored," Denise muttered.

"Shut up, Denise," Parker said as he glared back her.

"I'll never shut up at the kind of things you've done throughout our marriage!"

"Then get up and leave. You know where the door is," Parker said.

Nigel sighed. "And I'm gonna leave if the two of you don't stop. This is why I don't like having dinner with only the two of you."

"Well, too bad. We're your parents," Denise said.

"That's right," Parker added.

Nigel's phone rang. He looked at it to see who was calling him and put it back in his pocket.

It was Lisa.

"Who was it, dear?" Denise asked.

"No one," Nigel replied.

"I hope you're saying that about a woman and not about your business associates and lawyers," Parker said.

Nigel laughed. "Like father, like son."

They both laughed as Denise shook her head in disgust.

"Yeah, because the whole world knows you had a lot of fun in your early years," Denise said.

"And in my later years," Parker replied with a laugh, and took a sip of his drink. "I'm always gonna have fun."

"Don't even start," Denise warned. "You don't wanna make me upset here at the dinner table more than you already have."

"You're always upset," Parker said with a grin. "You've always lived this life and it's like you still can't be happy about anything. I don't know what the hell your problem is all the time."

Nigel looked at her with a huge grin.

"Do you really want me to answer that?" she asked.

"Nope, because I don't wanna hear it," Parker replied, and continued to eat.

"Can we just get through this dinner without arguing anymore, okay? I think we've talked enough about the women that I have kids by. I had nothing to do with what'd happened between Ivy and Taylor, so there's nothing more to say about it. I'm a grown man and make my own decisions, and Ivy made hers and now she's gonna be in prison probably for life for what she did to Taylor. I got enough to deal with when it comes to Aisha and this divorce we're going through."

"My advice is to try and work things out with Aisha, Nigel. It just doesn't look good for the two of you to divorce," Denise said.

"Sorry, Mom, but my mind is already made up."

"I agree with your mom, Nigel. But it's your life so suit yourself."

"Thanks for respecting my decision," he said. "Excuse me, I have to use the bathroom."

"And you come right back here and finish your dinner. Don't walk out that front door," Denise said with a smile.

Parker laughed with a nod as he chewed his food.

"I'll be right back, Mom, I promise," he replied.

He went to the bathroom, handled his business, and got on his phone.

"Nigel! Hi!" Lisa said with surprise since she didn't expect for him to call her back so soon.

"Hey, Lisa. I wanted to know if you still wanted to see me."

She grinned since she knew that he knew that was why she was calling him. "Of course."

"Cool. I'm at my parents' house having dinner so meet me at mine in about an hour, okay?"

"I'll be there."

CHAPTER FIFTEEN

"Glad to be out of there. My parents are something else," Nigel said, as he handed Lisa her usual bottle of water.

"Thank you," she replied with a smile as she sat on his couch in the family room. "But they seem like very nice people. It's clear they raised a gorgeous man who knows how to make and pass down generational wealth."

He nodded with a smile as he sat down in his favorite chair. "Yeah, I'll say they did good in that aspect. I'm the only child they have *in* wedlock. My dad had a lot of fun outside of his marriage to my mom, and it resulted in a lot children, but none of them can own any of the businesses. All of the businesses are in my name and are in my parents' wills. My mom doesn't want any of his kids anywhere near anything that has to do with our family name."

"Wow. I don't know what to say except that in a lot of ways I don't blame her."

"Neither do I. Not trying to be selfish, but they don't deserve anything. They have different mothers and my dad was never married to any of them since he's been married to my mom for more than fifty years. I didn't come along until ten years into their marriage, so I have some older brothers and sisters. I'm only forty. The youngest one, I believe, is only in her twenties."

"My goodness," she said as she shook her head. "Does he at least see them and give them money if they need it?"

"Of course, but like I said, they can't own any of the Foreman businesses. Some have started their own, I heard. All I care about is my family's businesses because that's how I keep my kids wealthy and I want that for generations to come."

"What did Aisha think of you having so many kids out of wedlock?"

He gave her a smirk. "C'mon, Lisa. What kind of a question is that? My cheating is one of the main reasons why we're divorcing, and I can't blame her for hating me because of it. I fathered four kids outside of our marriage, and she acts like my mom about not letting them be a part of anything that has to do with the Foreman family. Hell, she doesn't even want them to know their half-siblings."

"But how do *you* feel about it?"

"I honestly don't care. They're all being taken care of—all nine of them—so Aisha nor my surviving baby mamas have nothing to complain about, even though Ivy ain't getting shit anymore because her ass is going to prison if she's convicted."

What a mess, she thought.

"So, did your parents want you to give that press conference today?"

"Yeah, they did. They said it would look good for me and the Foreman family to make a statement. They know I had nothing to do with what'd happened to Taylor so they knew not to even ask me about that."

She smiled. "I'm glad they believe in your innocence."

"Yeah, me too. Because like I said, I had nothing to do with it. Even my dad said these women are crazy out here."

She laughed. "Yeah, crazy for you."

He smiled with a nod. "Hey, what can I say?"

They stared at each other.

"So, where did you tell your husband you were going?" he asked, and then took a sip of his drink.

"I didn't have to tell him anything. He has a late meeting so I should be home in time before he gets home."

He grinned. "Yeah, when Aisha and I were married, I had a lot of those 'late meetings.'"

She gave him a look of suspicion. "Why do you say it like that?"

He shrugged. "You know what it is, Lisa. I know you're a smart woman."

She sighed. "Yeah, I know. I just don't have any proof that he's cheating on me, that's all. I have asked him—believe me, I have—and he told me he wasn't. I just don't know what to believe."

"Believe that he is, that's all I gotta say."

She sighed once again as she shook her head. "I really don't want to."

"Well, suit yourself, then. I'm just telling you the reality of it all."

The reality of it all. Did I really wanna know the reality of it all? she thought.

"What if he is cheating on you, Lisa? What will you do?"

She shook her head. "Well, I don't wanna lose him so nothing, I guess. Especially if I don't have any proof."

"What if you do have proof?"

"Then we'll have to go to marriage counseling. And if the counseling doesn't help and he doesn't stop then I would have to leave him. But if he did it only once and I could erase that one time then I would stay with him because he's not perfect. I can't let one mistake erase ten years of our marriage."

"Wow, I wish I had a wife like you."

She blushed. "That's very nice of you to say, Nigel."

He sized her up. "I mean it."

"Greg?" Lisa said, as she walked up the dark staircase to their bedroom. She didn't see any lights on once she reached the top floor.

She made it to their bedroom and turned on the lights. "Greg?"

She heard the toilet flush from the master bathroom; she grinned.

Greg emerged from the bathroom as he put his phone back in his pocket. "Hey, baby."

"Hi," she replied with a genuine smile. "How was the meeting?"

"Long and boring. Where were you? Out joy riding again?"

"Yes," she lied with a smile.

He came closer to her and began kissing her; she knew what he wanted this to lead to.

Minutes later, they laid in bed after making love.

"Just what I needed after a long day," he said with a smile as he had his arm around her.

"You know I'm willing to give you whatever you want."

He gave her a grin. "Are you really?"

"Yes, I am, Greg. You know that."

"Yeah, baby, I know. But when is this gonna happen for us?"

She started to get angry. "Greg, come on. We just got through making love. Each time we do this there's a chance I can end up pregnant. I don't think it's because I'm too old. I know I'm in my mid-to-late thirties, and there are millions of women having babies for the first time at my age, even a lot older than me."

He sighed. "I know, baby, but I just want this to happen for *us*." He looked at his phone. "I gotta take this call and I need to go to my den and look something up. See you later." He put back on his loungewear and left the room.

She continued to lay in bed as she stared up at the ceiling. She was jolted out of her thoughts by a text on her phone:

Hi, are you Lisa Everett?

She looked at the door to see if Greg was coming back in the room. She texted the person back:

Yes, I'm Lisa Everett. Who is this? I don't recognize the number.

Hi, Lisa. You don't know me, but I need to talk to you. My name is

Kayla Scott. I'm Parker Foreman's youngest daughter and Nigel Foreman's half-sister.

She gasped in shock!

OMG, hi, Kayla. I think it's important for us to talk as well. Where do you wanna meet?

I'll let you pick the place. Anywhere is fine with me. I'm off work for the next couple of days.

She picked the place where her and Nigel met. She texted Kayla back with the information.

Great, Lisa. I'll meet you there. You don't wanna miss what I have to say.

I'll be there, Kayla.

CHAPTER SIXTEEN

"Mmmm, these cupcakes are so good. Never had anything like them. Thanks for this rare treat," Kayla said as she sat across from Lisa at the bakery that she met Nigel in.

"No problem, Kayla. I feel it's a treat as well so that's why I only come here a few times a month."

She kept staring at her. She saw Nigel in her, but could see just by her appearance that she didn't live the life that her half-older brother lived. She definitely seemed to have lived more modestly, and it was clear that Nigel meant what he'd said about his half-siblings not having any part of the Foreman lifestyle.

"So, Kayla. I couldn't even sleep last night because I was waiting to meet with you today. I'm very curious to know what it is that you said I didn't wanna miss."

"Oh, yeah, of course," Kayla said, and then wiped her fingers off with a napkin and took a sip of her drink. "Well, as you know, I'm one of the daughters of Parker Foreman, Nigel's dad. My mom had an affair with him over twenty years ago—twenty-six years to be exact—and as a result, I was born."

"And I have to say that you look like Nigel. It's clear he was right about how many affairs his dad had."

"Yeah, my mom told me he had too many to count which resulted in at least ten kids, maybe more. I may not even be the youngest. For some reason, I don't think I am."

"Wow, him and his dad really created a big mess for themselves. But at least you all have been taken care of, right?"

"Only up until we were eighteen, Lisa. After that, my mom and I were on our own. My dad provided very well for us, but my mom squandered all of the money on luxury things and now we really have nothing to show for. My dad told her that he meant what he said about cutting us off when I was eighteen so she was forced to get a job and she has been working ever since and I've been working since I was eighteen, but it's just not enough, believe me."

Lisa shook her head. "I'm sorry to hear this, Kayla. I've been talking to Nigel only for a while now and he told me about all of you and how his mom doesn't want any of his dad's out-of-wedlock children to have anything. I just don't think that's right. They're his children, not hers."

"Yeah, Denise is a bitch. I can't stand her. She lives better than almost everyone in this world and all she cares about is still living that way. In a lot of ways I don't blame her, but all of his cheating didn't make her leave him so it shows just how much insecurity she has.

"My mom thought my dad was gonna leave her for her—I think she knows by now that it's never gonna happen. He was in his 50s and she was in her 30s when they got together. She told me it was a brief affair, but it ended in something lifelong when my mom got pregnant with me. He told her he would give her money but to never put him on child support or else she wasn't gonna get anything. He also told her that I could never inherit any of the businesses he owns and that went for all of his out-of-wedlock children; something about how his dad had that in his will and he had to honor it. Nigel is the only child he had with Denise, so everything is his."

"I don't think that's fair, Kayla, not at all. He's your biological dad, not even a stepdad or whatever. He has no right to treat you all like you're some outsiders."

"Well, I actually don't think it's him, I think it's Denise's influence, as well as Nigel's. Nigel's an asshole, Lisa. I'm telling you that right now. He acts just like his dad. You see how many kids he's fathered outside of his marriage to Aisha, so he didn't learn shit from his dad about what not to do."

"Yeah, everyone knows that. I admit that I've talked to him a lot, and he doesn't seem like the nicest person, but I just don't see any harm in talking to him because he doesn't treat me bad at all. He hasn't said anything bad about his out-of-wedlock half-siblings just so you know."

"He's talked a lot of shit about us, Lisa, he's just trying not to look bad in front of you."

"You think so?"

"Yes, I do."

"Well, then if you say it I believe it."

She sighed as she stared down at one of her cupcakes. "My mom and I are really struggling. And I've reached out to my dad and let him know it, but he said we've gotten all what we're gonna get from him so we're just gonna have to do the best we can, and that my mom should've saved and invested the money he'd given her for the first eighteen years of my life. I couldn't argue with that.

"I also reached out to Nigel for help, and he said he couldn't do anything for me as well and that he stands by what his dad told me. He said that if he helped me then he's helping my mom and he will have to help his other half-siblings and their moms as well and he wasn't gonna do that, so yeah, we're on our own."

Lisa shook her head. "This is really sad to listen to, Kayla. I think Nigel and his dad are very selfish people. And I don't have a good impression of his mom at all. She has every reason to be upset at her husband's numerous affairs resulting in a number of children, but it's not your fault or your other half-siblings' faults, either. Some people will never get over things and I'm not saying that they should. But it's not even her money. She's being selfish about money she never earned."

Kayla laughed. "Yeah, that's what everyone is saying, but she's his wife so she's legally entitled to everything of his and can make certain decisions if she wants. That's the power of being a wife, I guess. Something that my mom will probably never know about because she's never been married, and men don't seem to want to marry her because they know she had me by Parker. They see her as some old thot now."

"That's not right," Lisa said, and then took a sip of her drink. "Since I'm married, I know personally that I will not be happy if my husband fathered a child outside of our marriage. I just don't think Denise's madness all of these years should be taken out on the kids her husband had by those women. They're human beings. You all didn't ask to come into this world under the circumstances that you all did. I feel like she's punishing you all, and especially y'alls mothers."

"Yeah, that's exactly how I feel and a lot of my half-siblings feel the same way as well as their mothers. It's not right, but what can we say? All I can do at this point is try the best I can and hope to be married someday like you, Lisa. I told my mom that the last thing I wanted to do was end up like her, and she agreed with me. She said she wants something better for me and wants to make sure I get it. But she also confessed something to me."

Lisa's eyes got big. "What was it?"

"That she was never attracted to my dad. She didn't like older men at all but thought that since she was young and beautiful that she could take my dad away from his wife so she could replace her and live that fairytale life. And she really thought that after she found out she was pregnant with me. She had an affair with a rich man, had me, and he *never* left his wife for her. And now she's broke, we're broke, and struggling. It's a tough life for us now, but I don't intend for it to be like this forever.

"You seem to have it all, Lisa, and I admire you for it. I know nothing and no one is perfect, but what you have is what I want. No woman would wanna go through what my mom and I are going through just because she thought she was gonna live some lavish lifestyle with a married man once he divorced his wife. It never happened.

"You know, I tell every woman who has asked me about Nigel's divorce from Aisha that he's not worth being with and that he's just like his dad. It's unbelievable how much a man can end up like his father, and not in a good way. I tell them they're better off finding a man who will truly love them and respect them, and to leave men like Nigel alone because he's just not worth being with —don't know how many times I have to say it. I tell them they don't wanna end up like my mom and me and all of the other women who my dad had fathered kids with. He acts as if Nigel is his only child, just like how Nigel acts like his five kids by Aisha are his only children.

"It sucks to be a child out-of-wedlock, Lisa, it really does. Because of the staggering wealth that my dad has, I feel like I've already missed out on a lifetime of having a fabulous lifestyle where I don't have to worry about working dead-end jobs and not being able to pay bills and being able to do whatever I want when I want and just living my dreams. But this is my reality, and unless I end up getting married to a man who has the kind of wealth like my dad, it will always be a reality for me."

Lisa shook her head as she wrote in her diary later on that day:

> I met with Kayla, Nigel's youngest half-sister by his dad. I can't believe the things she'd told me, and let me tell you, they have stuck to me; can't stop thinking about them. I see just how lucky I am to have someone like Greg and how important marriage and having a structured family really is.

I feel so sorry for Kayla, but I didn't wanna tell her that this was her mom's fault just as much as her dad's because they put her in that situation—but judging by what she'd told me, she already knows that. She even told me that Nigel doesn't give her shit just as much as her dad doesn't anymore and talks shit about her and his other half-siblings, and I just think they're being selfish and because of this, Nigel is looking less and less desirable to even talk to no matter what he considers me since he said he has no female friends.

I don't think any woman would wanna end up like how Kayla and her mom did, and I know it's not just her, it's all of her dad's out-of-wedlock child's moms who are in this position. I guess it was worse than I thought and Nigel followed right in his dad's messy footsteps and created a big-ass mess of his own. I think their mess is gonna get a lot worse and I want no part of any of it.

Kayla said I had it all, but I beg to differ. My life just isn't as perfect as she thinks it is, but by what she'd told me today, I can see how she would wanna trade places with me. If I was in her position I would want to as well because it's better than how she's living at this moment. And it really hurt to think about the extravagant lifestyle that she knows her and her other half-siblings have missed out on so far in their lives just because of their dad fathering them outside of his marriage. I honestly thought Nigel was kidding when he said they weren't gonna get anything and weren't a part of anything that had to do with the Foreman fortune . . . until Kayla confirmed this very unfortunate truth.

I do feel very fortunate and lucky to live the life I live because things could be a lot worse for me. I didn't wanna tell Kayla that Nigel and I have gotten physical with each other because

I felt that it was none of her business and it's just something she didn't need to know. But I feel she told me a lot of things that I needed to know about him, and in a lot of ways she was warning me that I shouldn't try and get too close to him, even though she didn't come right out and say it.

Bitterness? Yes, of course. But no one can blame her for that.

"So, honey, did you do anything interesting today?" Greg asked, as he ate some of his chicken parmigiana.

"Yeah, as a matter of fact I did," Lisa replied, and then ate some of her salad. "I met up at my favorite bakery shop with a woman name Kayla."

"Kayla? Do I know her?" he asked, and then took a sip of his drink.

"No, I don't think you do, Greg."

"How do *you* know her?"

"Well, she contacted me last night by text. I had no idea who she was."

"How did she get your number if she didn't know you?"

She honestly forgot to ask Kayla this when she met up with her. "I honestly don't know. I forgot to ask her."

He gave her a look of confusion. "You met up with a woman who mysteriously texted you, Lisa? And you had no idea who she was? Are you crazy? I don't like the sound of this."

"Greg, it's okay. Because she told me in the text who she was and of course I had to find out in person if she was telling me the truth."

He sighed. "Who is she, Lisa?"

"Kayla Scott. She's the youngest half-sister of Nigel."

He dropped his fork and shook his head. "Should've known." He sighed as he shook his head once again. "And what the hell did she wanna talk to you for, Lisa? It's clear to me she wanted to talk to you about Nigel."

"Of course she did, Greg."

He sighed once again. "And?"

"And she's a really nice woman. Her and her mom are really struggling."

"Well, that's her mom's fault. She should've never fucked a married man and a had a kid by him. Things like that never turn out well, Lisa, any idiot knows that. Oh, let me guess? She wanted to tell her sad, sob story to you about how her dad never left his wife for her mom, right?"

She grinned. "Yeah, you're right, Greg. But you know none of this is Kayla's fault."

"And none of this is any of your business, Lisa. I don't know why you wanna be so up in all of this shit with that asshole and now you got one of his half-sisters texting you wanting to talk to you? You're not one of those gossip bloggers."

"I know I'm not."

"So there must be a lot that you're not telling me about you and your little friendship with Nigel because everyone knows you know him and it's clear to me that you're still talking to him."

She sighed. "Like I've said a million times, it seems, I just don't see any harm in it, Greg. He hasn't been disrespectful to me or anything. I have to admit she told me how he hasn't given her shit and that her dad cut her and her mom off when she was eighteen. She's twenty-six now."

"And how is any of this any concern of yours?"

"Because I care, that's all."

"I'm not saying that you shouldn't care, Lisa, I'm just saying that you have your own marriage and we're trying to start a family of our own. I know you get bored and lonely, but there are a million of other things you can do instead of being all caught up in the Nigel Foreman divorce-baby-mama-drama-half-siblings saga, and that goes for his dad as well. Never liked him, either, and neither do a lot of people. The whole Foreman family isn't likable, Lisa. I feel they're very condescending and look down on others who don't match their wealth, especially their own people."

"Come on, Greg. That's not fair to say. I've seen how they've helped our people a lot when it was needed. I mean, yes, they've been selfish about a lot of things, but they've done their share of good things as well."

"Not as much as they should. But I still don't understand why you feel you still have to talk to him all the time. You're not a part of his family, and as you know, they don't even want half-siblings to be a part of their family. Who acts like that?"

"I never said it was right, Greg, and I even told Kayla that. I think her and her other siblings should be a part of the Foreman family. They're missing out on a lifetime of an extravagant lifestyle all because of them being born outside of Nigel's parents' marriage. They really put Nigel up on a pedestal."

"And someone needs to knock it down. I saw—we both saw— who he really is that night that he tried to clown me in front of you, and now you tell me all of this stuff that Kayla told you. If you can't see any of this and respect me and our marriage by now by not talking to him anymore then I'm just at a loss, Lisa, I really am. I think there's a reason why Kayla wanted you to know how he really is and I feel she was warning you about something."

She stared at him in suspense. "Warning me about what?"

He glared at her as he chewed his food. He took a sip of his drink. "I don't know, Lisa. You tell me."

"There's nothing to tell, Greg, *I swear* there isn't."

He got up with his plate and drink. "I'm gonna finish this in my den. The game is about to start."

CHAPTER SEVENTEEN

The rain pounded down on the house the next day as Lisa sat by the
window as she wrote in her diary:

> Greg is mad at me again. I knew I should've never told him
> about me meeting up with Kayla yesterday. He just wants me
> to stop talking to Nigel and said that Kayla was trying to
> warn me about something obviously having to do with him.
> The only thing she warned me about was the kind of person I
> already know Nigel to be. I think she doesn't know much
> about him like the way she tried to make me believe, but
> what I do know is that her whole situation is sad and it's not
> her fault. I just hope she finds the happiness I feel she
> deserves because no one deserves what her and the rest of
> her half-siblings are going through, and no one would wanna
> go through any of that themselves, especially Nigel.

She was jolted out of her thoughts when her phone rang. She
picked it up.

It was Nigel.

"Nigel, hi."

"Hey, Lisa. We need to talk."

She didn't like the sound of this. "Okay. Is there something wrong?"

"It depends. I'm at one of my restaurants today so can you meet me here now?"

"Sure. What's the address?" She wrote it down. "Okay, I'll be there."

She walked into Nigel's office at Denise's, one of his more upscale restaurants named after his mom. And just like his office at his construction company, she could see the luxury all in it. "Hi, Nigel."

Nigel put down his *Departures* magazine. "Have a seat."

She nervously sat down. She could sense that he wasn't happy about something. "So, why did you wanna see me?"

"What were you doing meeting up with Kayla yesterday?"

She sighed. She knew he would find out one way or the other. "She texted me, Nigel. She told me she just wanted to talk."

"About what?" he asked as he glared at her.

"Um, just about her and how she was related to you."

"Yeah . . . and?"

"And that's about it, Nigel."

"You're lying, Lisa," he informed her as he kept his daunting glare on her. "That's not all she wanted. She doesn't know a thing about you and she especially doesn't know shit about me. What did she really talk about? Was she trying to turn you against me?"

"No, she wasn't. She just told me that the two of you are not close and that she wishes that you were."

"Yeah, only so she can get money."

"But don't you think she deserves something for being your half-sister?"

"No, none of them do. They don't deserve shit. Their mothers are whores for fucking around with my dad. Yeah, he's no angel, either, but they knew the deal. He was never gonna leave my mom for any of them. They couldn't take it for what it was. My dad has given all of them what he was gonna give them until they were eighteen, and I know damn well they're all past that age and some have been past that age for decades so they're on their own. They're not getting anything from him, me, or anyone in my family. They better be lucky they got what they got."

This is not right, she thought. "Well, she wasn't begging for anything, Nigel. She just told me that her and her mom are really struggling. How did you find out that I met up with her?"

"Social media, how do you think?"

"Well, I didn't say anything on social media about meeting up with her."

"But she obviously did. Look, if you wanna keep seeing me then you need to stop talking to her and not talk to any of my other half-siblings either. Got it?"

"Yeah, I got it," she said, as George Benson's "I Just Wanna Hang Around You" began playing.

He got up out of his seat as he stared at her, walking right past her to the door. She knew he wanted her to leave. She got up.

"Where are you going?"

"I . . . thought you wanted me to leave."

"Not yet," he informed her, and *locked the door.*

She felt herself go into a panic. "What's going on?"

"Relax, Lisa. I just want some privacy, that's all." He sat back down at his desk. "I love this song."

"Me too. It's old school, of course, and my parents were always listening to this music because it was popular in the eighties. It made me love it."

"And I love your company," he said with a smile.

She smiled big. "I'm very glad to hear that. Despite Greg not wanting me to talk to you much less see you, I just can't help it. I feel happier when I see you; not to say that Greg doesn't make me happy."

He nodded. "Glad to hear it, Lisa. You know I can make any woman happy. I can give her a life she can only dream of—free of loneliness, boredom, and financial worries. Only one woman knew how that was, and I say *was* because she blew it, not me. I know there's a better woman for me."

"There is, Nigel. And when you find her, maybe you'll change your mind about getting remarried."

He kept staring at her. "Maybe I will."

Anita Baker's "Good Love" was now playing.

"I can love any woman down, but whether she deserves the love I can give her is the question. Most don't deserve it. No man can give the kind of love I can give a woman."

She slowly stood up and walked over to him. Something unexplainable was taking over her at this moment. She stood in front of him.

He smiled at her as he remained seated. "So, why are you standing in front of me?"

She smiled as she kept staring down at him.

His smile got even bigger. "What are you waiting for? Give me all you got."

She got on him in a straddle position and they began kissing like they hadn't seen each other in years. She knew it was wrong, but she couldn't fight these feelings she was having for a man that were reserved for her husband. Never had she felt this way before.

They took off their pants and she slid down on him and he moved up and down as his chair was tilted back as far as it would go.

"Fuck that shit, baby," he repeated over and over again, and then pulled up her shirt, unhooked her bra, and started sucking on her tits.

She moaned in pleasure. "Never had it done this good before," she said as she breathed heavy.

"I'm the best," he informed her and continued on. "Get up, I wanna fuck you from behind."

She turned around and laid her arms on his desk as he went back inside of her and went at it fast and hard, and let out a very satisfying moan as he pulled out of her.

He went into his private bathroom where she heard the toilet flush a minute later. "I have a meeting here in about a half hour. Did you want some takeout?"

"Sure, I would love that. I've never had any food from here before and I heard it was great but very expensive. Can I get some for Greg?"

He smirked. "Yeah, that's fine."

She started to feel guilty about cheating on him once again. "Um, you're not gonna tell anyone about this since I'm married?"

"Why would I do that? It's no one's business what we do. I'm still technically married as well since I'm not officially divorced. If you wanna do it again let me know."

She stared at him. She knew she should not have done this, but there was no way she could take back what'd happened. "How much do I owe you for the food?"

"Nothing. It's complimentary. You were great," he said with sly smile.

She nodded with her head down, trying to hide the shame she'd felt for officially having sex with a man other than her husband. "Thank you."

CHAPTER EIGHTEEN

"This is delicious, honey. Reminds me of the restaurant George that we went to on one of our many trips to London," Greg said, as he ate the food that Lisa had gotten from Nigel.

"It does," she reminisced with a smile as she sat across from him. "That's what I thought of, too."

"Where is this from?"

"Richard's," she lied, since it had similar food like Denise's.

"Sounds good. I heard about it but I've never been there. We'll have to put it on the list for one of our date nights."

"Yeah, we do," she nervously replied.

"It also tastes a lot like Denise's, and the reason why I know is because one of my colleagues wanted it for her birthday so that's what we had brought in. But you know how I feel about anything having to do with Nigel Foreman. This was obviously before you met him."

She felt herself go into a panic. "I know, honey. Let's not talk about him, okay? Let's just enjoy this food."

"Hey, fine with me," he replied, and continued eating.

Several minutes later while Greg was in his den doing work, she sat in the family room and wrote an entry in her diary:

I can't believe I did it. Yes, I did *that*. I ate the forbidden fruit, no pun intended. Luckily, he did wear a condom. I think his drawers are stuffed with them in all of his offices—or at least they should be, but you never know because of all of those kids he has—but I didn't know he was gonna use one of them on me.

I can't believe I had sex outside of my marriage.

I've never done anything like this before. I did not expect for this to go as far as it did with Nigel. He gave me the food from his restaurant for free and even said I could get some for Greg; hinting to me that I was getting it for free because I was great. God, I feel awful, just awful. There is no way I can take back what I've done. Nigel told me that he can love any woman down and can give her a life that she's dreamed of. I don't doubt it at all, but I won't ever be a part of that because I'm married, but if Greg finds out what I did then I know my marriage will probably be over, but I will try my best to save it as much as I can.

I made a mistake. I got caught up. I felt like I was a different person doing what I did with him. Something took over me today, I hate to say, and I just can't ever let it happen again.

She got up to go do the laundry that she held off doing earlier today. She emptied Greg's pockets out of the clothes he needed washed . . . .

And out fell a gold hoop earring from his work pants!

She picked it up off the floor and held it in her hands. She sighed as tears welled up in her eyes. She knew this earring was not hers. She put it in her pocket and continued on sorting out the clothes.

Several minutes later, she got on the phone and called Sharita.

"Lisa, hey. What's up, girl?"

"A lot. I just can't tell you over the phone. I need to talk to you in person as soon as possible."

"Oh, shit! What's the matter? Why can't you tell me right now?"

"Because I just can't," she said, as tears once again welled up in her eyes. "Can I come over there now?"

"Lisa, you sound like you're about to start crying. What's wrong?"

"I . . . I can't say over the phone, Sharita."

"Does it have to do with what I think it has to do with?"

"Yes, and a lot more."

"Okay. Come on over."

CHAPTER NINETEEN

 table. She shook her head. "So, how long do you think he's been cheating on you?"

"I have no idea," Lisa said, as she patted her eyes. "I know he didn't just find it on the floor where he works at because he would've returned it to the front reception area in case the woman came back looking for it. It's clear he's seeing this woman."

"Do you have any idea who it might be?"

She shrugged. "I honestly don't know. It can be anyone. Greg is gorgeous. He's definitely one of those doctors that grab all the attention from nurses, other female doctors, and especially patients. I just don't know what to do."

"Confront him about it, Lisa. You have to do it. You have to let him know that you're on to him."

"Like how he's on to me about Nigel."

"But he has no proof that you've been seeing Nigel even though he told you not to. You're his wife, not some girlfriend or some woman he's just seeing. You should not be afraid to talk to him and especially about something like this."

"I know. But if he is officially cheating on me, Sharita, I can't say anything now."

Sharita's mouth dropped. "Oh no, Lisa! Don't tell me—"

"That I had sex with Nigel? Yeah, I did. I did it this afternoon in his office at one of his restaurants. I feel so awful."

"Lisa! Oh, shit! What the hell? Now I'm not gonna lie, I never thought you would actually have sex with another man outside of your marriage."

"I never thought I would either, but I did and there's nothing no one can say to me to make me feel better about it. I made a *big* mistake. But then later when I get home and after Greg and I were done eating, I started on the laundry and there out pops that earring. It's like I couldn't believe what I was seeing. I felt it was instant karma that I cheated on him with Nigel and then I find evidence that he could be doing the same to me—of all times I find this, you know?"

"Yeah, this is pretty fucked up. But *please* tell me Nigel used a condom?"

"Of course. After we were done he pulled it off as he walked to his bathroom inside of his office. I still feel so bad."

"Well, something would be wrong with you if you *didn't* feel bad about it, Lisa. But I think you and Greg really need to sit down and have an honest talk with each other, and if he admits to you that he has been cheating on you then you need to admit that you've been cheating on him as well. It's only fair."

She sighed as she stared down at her cup of coffee. "Yeah, you're right. It's only fair." She got up and paced around in the kitchen. "I just don't know why Greg would do this to me if he is, and I can't shake the fact that he is. I know he's been upset about the fact that I haven't gotten pregnant yet, but that doesn't mean he has to go running into the arms of another woman because of it and fucking her. I just don't know what to think about anything anymore. Sometimes I do wonder if we were really meant to be together."

"Lisa, are you serious? You're sounding like a whole different person now."

"And I felt like a different person when Nigel and I were having sex. He said he can give any woman the life she really wants."

"Yeah, and you know he says that to every woman he sees, Lisa. I know that you know better not to get caught up in that shit like what all of those other women got caught up in, especially those three that had kids by him when he was married and he still is married since his divorce is obviously not finalized yet."

"I know, Sharita. I'm no fool, believe me. Unlike them, obviously, I regretted it the second we were done. I'm very aware of the way Nigel is and no woman should expect for him to only wanna be with her, and especially now since he's getting a divorce. I'm very lucky to be married, but for today I was one stupid woman who disrespected my marriage vows and had sex with another man, and now I have evidence that Greg probably did the same to me."

"And it's up to the two of you to talk this out and save your marriage. I think the two of you were made for each other, but neither one of you are perfect and make mistakes like what we all do. Talk to him soon, Lisa, because the longer you hold off on this the harder it's gonna be."

"Yeah, I know."

CHAPTER TWENTY

GREG WALKED INTO THE KITCHEN FROM THE GARAGE AND TURNED ON THE lights . . . and found Lisa sitting at the island counter. "Lisa? What's wrong? Why are you sitting here in the dark?"

She gave him a blank stare.

He walked over to her. "Lisa, what the hell is wrong? Why aren't you dressed for our date night tonight?"

"Because I don't think we should go tonight because of what we need to talk about," she replied as she stared down at the counter. She pulled the gold hoop earring out of her pocket. "I don't think we'll make it through our date night out at a restaurant if I wanna talk about this."

He sighed and sat down next to her. "What about it, Lisa?"

"What about it, Greg?!" she snapped back. "Who the fuck does it belong to because it definitely doesn't belong to me!"

"If you don't calm down right now then I'm not gonna have this conversation with you. I'll walk right back out that door and get my own damn dinner. I wanna eat in peace and was looking forward to a nice night tonight."

"Oh, so you think we shouldn't talk about this, huh? You think I should just ignore what fell out of your pants while I was sorting clothes to do the laundry, huh? Whose earring is this, Greg?"

He shook his head. "It doesn't matter, Lisa. I love you, okay? We shouldn't make a big deal out of this."

"The fuck we shouldn't!" she yelled as tears welled up in her eyes. "You obviously don't love me that much since you cheated on me, Greg! And you're not even fuckin' man enough to admit it to me! You're gonna sit here and lie to my fuckin' face about not cheating on me? Are you really gonna do that, Greg?"

"Stop all of your cussing right now. You know I don't like excessive cussing coming from you."

"Oh, but it's okay that you do it? It's okay that you can do anything you want because you're the one who built this lifestyle for us and have been the sole provider for us for over ten years, huh? And all I'm just supposed to do is act like a good little submissive, feminine housewife that doesn't cuss and doesn't do anything you don't want me to do!"

"What have you been doing that I don't want you to do, Lisa? Huh? Since you brought it up. Why don't we get all of this fuckin' shit out in the open right now." He walked over to the refrigerator and got himself an energy drink. "So, talk. I wanna hear everything. It's clear that you wanna talk about this shit so talk about it, I'm listening!"

"Don't yell at me!"

He laughed and then took a sip of his drink. "Oh, okay! So you can yell at me and accuse me of cheating when the only proof you think you have is an overpriced, funky-ass gold hoop earring you found in my pants pocket. How do I know you didn't plant it there yourself and is trying to set me up for something?"

"Set you up, Greg? *Set you up*?! Now you're sounding fuckin' ridiculous! I didn't set you up for shit so shut the fuck up about that! How the fuck did it get there, Greg? How? It didn't just put itself in there, I know it! You know damn well you're fucking whosever earring this is!"

"Are you fucking Nigel Foreman?"

She gasped! "And like what you just asked me, Greg, what kind of proof do you have that I am?"

He shook his head. "None, and I'm man enough to admit it, Lisa. But if you're fucking him and I find out that you are, you're in big trouble, more than you ever know."

"*Don't* threaten me, Greg! That's something I won't tolerate!"

"Then don't ever lie to me when I ask you about him. I'm serious, Lisa. Only you know if you're fucking him. At this point I don't care if you've done it once or several times, if I find proof that you did then like I said, you're gonna be sorry you did."

"Oh, what the fuck are you gonna do to me, Greg? Kill me?" she asked as tears streamed down from her eyes.

"Now you're being absolutely ridiculous, Lisa. Killing you for cheating on me never even crossed my mind. Only men who feel like they have nothing else to live for will do some shit like that. I'm not that type of man and you know it. Just don't let me find proof that you've cheated on me with him, that's all I'm saying." He grabbed his keys off the counter. "I'm gonna go get something to eat. You're on your own."

She continued to breathe heavy as she tried to calm herself down. Her phone chimed in with a text:

Looks like you and Nigel had a lot of fun this afternoon.

She looked at the video thumbnail that showed Nigel and her having sex in his office!

Greg stared at her. "Who is it?"

"Chassy," she calmly replied.

He made his way to the door and left out of it.

Tears welled back up in her eyes. She had no idea who had sent this to her since it came in as ANONYMOUS. She clicked on the video and saw for herself that someone had this on video. She couldn't believe this was happening.

Another text came in:

$100K and this will all go away.

She texted the person back:

I don't have $100K! Who the hell are you? You have no right to black-mail me like this!

She breathed heavy as she waited for a response. It came in seconds later.

No $100K? Oh well, then a copy of this will be texted to your husband. And as you see, I have proof that I have his number."

She shook her head as Greg's number stared back at her from this person's text.

Have a nice day!

She went into a panic and texted the person back:

Wait! I'll try to come up with it! Please, I need time! Please!

Okay, I'll give you time, but not as much as you think so get it together as fast as you can.

CHAPTER TWENTY-ONE

"So, Lisa, what brings you here? You sounded as if you were in a full-blown panic on the phone?" Nigel asked, as he sat at his desk in his office at his construction company. "I can see that something is wrong by your appearance." He sized up her disheveled look in a hoodie, ripped jeans, and dirty sneakers with her hair in a messy bun along with not a stitch of makeup on.

"I'm in a lot of trouble, Nigel," she nervously said as she stood in front of his desk.

"Calm down and have a seat. I want you to relax when you're here."

She sat down fast but at the edge of the seat. "I can't waste any time. Someone has us on video having sex in your office at your restaurant."

"Is this a joke?" he asked as he stared at her.

"No, it's *not,* Nigel!" she said as tears welled up in her eyes. She quickly grabbed a tissue off of his desk and patted her eyes with it. "Greg and I got into a big fight last night because I found a woman's earring in the pocket of his work pants and confronted him about it. He never admitted to me that he was cheating on me and I never admitted to cheating on him; we didn't get anywhere. And he flat-out asked me was I fucking you."

He grinned. "And I take it you said you weren't."

"What was I supposed to say?"

"What you said. I'm not mad at you, Lisa. So, what brings you here?"

"He said if he found proof that I'm cheating on him then I was in big trouble. He threatened me, Nigel! He's never threatened me before! He said he wouldn't kill me but at this point I just don't know what he's thinking. It's like he can see right through me and that scares me! I think he knows that I cheated on him with you and it's like he's knows I've done it more than once."

"But it's okay for him to do it to you, huh?"

"Yeah, that's the way he wanted to make it seem but he never admitted to me that he is; said I have no proof that he is just like I said he has no proof of me cheating on him with you . . . but now he will! And the person showed proof that they will send it to him because they have his phone number and I don't know how the hell they got mine much less his!"

He sat up in his chair. "What are you talking about?"

"*This!*" she said, and handed her phone to him.

He looked at it and shook his head. "I'm sorry about this, Lisa. I actually thought you were kidding at first when you said someone had us on video having sex in one of my offices. It's obvious someone planted a camera in there to catch me doing something, probably Aisha when we were together."

"So you didn't know about any cameras in your office?"

"Just the company cameras, but I can tell by the angle that's not the company camera. This is a personal one."

She wiped tears from her eyes. "Look at the text that was sent along with the video."

He read them and shook his head. "So, you need $100,000 and they won't send this to your husband, huh?"

"That's what they said, but I just don't know! I don't have this kind of money, Nigel! I don't know why they're doing this to me! Has anyone contacted you about this?"

"No, no one has," he honestly replied. "I have no idea who could've sent this; very hard to tell since I know a ton of people and they know people, so you know how it is."

She sighed as she stared up at the ceiling as tears still streamed from her eyes. Her eyes came off the ceiling and met his. "*Please*, Nigel. I've never asked for anything. I don't want Greg finding out about this. *Please*. I know it'll take me a long time to pay you back but you'll get your money back. I just don't know anyone else that has the kind of money you have. I need to save my marriage to Greg. This is not worth it ending over. I need your help more than anything now. We both did this but they're only blackmailing me about it. I just wanna get this over with and move on from it."

He continued to stare at her. "What's in it for me?"

CHAPTER TWENTY-TWO

Cold, alone, and indescribably afraid, Lisa stood in the dark out in the middle of nowhere with only the lights from her SUV beaming down an endless path of darkness, as she held a suitcase with $100,000 in cash, courtesy of Nigel. He told her she didn't have to pay him back for the money that he'd given her since he was involved in what had gotten her in this trouble to begin with, but she felt she was indebted to him forever for it.

She jumped at the chime of her phone.

Be there in a minute.

The blackmailer.

She sighed as her body shook out of pure fear. She had no one with her. No one on her side. No one knew she was here except Nigel and the blackmailer. She wanted Nigel to come with her at the very least for her protection, but he told her he didn't want any part of it.

Faint lights appeared before her that looked like they were miles ahead.

Seconds later, they grew into a set of headlights that came right at her, and the black SUV with dark tinted windows slowed down several feet in front of her.

The blackmailer was here.

She shook even more as the suitcase vibrated off of her right leg. Never did she ever think she would be in a situation where she would be standing at the end of a dark, deserted road at night with the only lights coming from the headlights of cars, and especially carrying a suitcase full of cash from a man she cheated on her husband with. She felt like she was in some dark romance movie.

Two men got out of the SUV, one from the driver's side and one from the passenger's side.

Two.

Two against one.

Both of the men were about the same size and height and looked like NFL linebackers. They wore ski masks and dark clothes since it was obvious they didn't want to be identified.

She felt like dropping the suitcase, jumping into her car and driving off.

"Lisa?" the man who got out on the driver's side asked.

"Yes?" she squeaked back.

"I see you got something for us," the man on the passenger's side said.

"Yes," she squeaked out once again.

"Stay where you are. Put the suitcase on the ground and shove it over to me," the man on the passenger's side instructed.

She did what he said. She was relieved to get the suitcase out of her hands and away from her as much as possible.

The man on the passenger's side bent down and opened up the suitcase, and made sure that all $100,000 of the money was in fact there. "Good girl," he said, and closed the suitcase. He slowly got up. "Now you don't have to—"

Pop!

Pop! Pop! Pop!

He fell to the ground as the suitcase dropped out of his hand!

Lisa screamed in horror! She looked at the man who got out of the driver's side.

He put his gun back in his holster and walked over to the suitcase and picked it up, as well as the blackmailer's phone and put it in his pocket. "Sorry you had to see that. Courtesy of the High-Nine-Figure Man," he informed her.

Her mouth dropped in shock!

Nigel was behind this! Oh, my God! she thought, as she still stood in complete shock at what she'd just witnessed.

"You're okay, Lisa. Don't worry about a thing. You weren't here tonight. This never happened. Go on home to your husband."

"Wha . . . what about . . . *him*?" she asked as she shook uncontrollably.

"What about him?" he asked. "He stays where he lays, but someone will eventually find him. He learned his lesson the hard way. Go on home. Goodnight," he said, and walked back to the SUV with the suitcase.

She got back in her SUV as the blackmailer's body laid lifeless in the middle of the road. She knew he was dead. She drove off and the man in the SUV followed behind her for a while, and then made a right turn some few miles from where she'd witnessed a man be executed right in front of her.

And Nigel was behind it all.

She started to hyperventilate and began to cry uncontrollably, knowing that this was all because of her.

Several minutes later, she walked into her house and it was as dark as the road she'd witnessed an unexpected murder on. She walked upstairs and could hear Greg talking on his phone in his den. She went straight to it and peeked in on him. He didn't even look at her.

She sighed and went back to their room and took a shower, wishing that she could wash away every single thing that'd happened since she'd met Nigel. She knew the blackmailer was dead, and as his killer said, he learned his lesson the hard way. But he was dead because of her, she'd felt, and she would always feel bad about it.

She took out her computer and wrote in her diary:

I'm gonna take what I saw tonight to my grave. Never did I ever think I would ever be involved in something like this. You see this shit on TV all the time, but when it happens to you it's on a whole other level. I just can't believe this. And Nigel was behind it all. It was clear the blackmailer was set up and Nigel was not gonna give any of his money to him over a sex video, and he was obviously right about knowing a lot of people because how would the driver know the black-mailer since the driver clearly worked for Nigel?

Was Nigel really protecting me or was he really all about protecting his money and himself?

I have to talk to him about this ASAP. I know that he knows by now what'd happened, and I can't believe that this happened because of something I chose to do—have sex with another man outside of my marriage. Greg has no idea what I witnessed and he's never—

Her phone rang.
Nigel.
She picked it up. "Hello?"
"Hey. Got time to see me?"
"Of course."
"You can come on over to my house. Don't worry, I'm here alone."
"Um . . . okay, I'll be right there."
She got her purse and went to the den once again to peek in on Greg. He looked at her, turned back towards the TV, and continued talking on the phone.

. . .

"That punk has been trying to extort money from me forever, it seems. Good riddance. He should've known he was gonna get his someday and he did. He knew by going after you for that amount that you would come to me to get it and you did exactly what he thought you'd do, but now the joke is on him because he's dead and I still got all of my money."

"I can't believe what I'd witnessed, Nigel! I'm still shaking from it!"

"Relax, it's okay. Your marriage is officially saved without you having to pay him a dime for threatening to expose our affair. But you know you can't tell anyone what you witnessed. My man doesn't need to go to prison because of it. I wanna protect him and of course you know I protected you."

"And I can't thank you enough for it. I just didn't think anyone would die over it."

"Well, I agree that it didn't have to come to that, but that punk was asking for it for a while. Like I said, he's been trying to extort money from me for years and not only that, just constantly disrespecting me on social media as well. I didn't have to take that shit from him anymore. He learned his lesson today the hard way. My men warned him in so many ways that he was gonna learn one day and he didn't listen, and this is what happens when you don't listen and you think you can do what you wanna do and not care what people say."

"People should know not to cross you."

"Exactly, and look what happens when they do. You personally saw that."

"And there's no way I can unsee it. I still can't believe I witnessed it. I never thought in my life that I would be in that situation, you know? Giving money to someone so they wouldn't expose an affair I'm having—and that much money at that—and then see the person get killed by the person who drove them there to get the money from me. It was too much, Nigel, it really was."

"That's because you saw someone learn their life's lesson right in front of you. Too bad it had to be a deadly one but hey, like I said, he was asking for it for a while. Life is a lesson and he failed that lesson miserably. People just don't know when to stop their shit, so he had to pay for it with his life."

She didn't wanna ask the next question, but she had to know. "Um, has anyone else out there learned their lesson from you?"

"You mean have I had anyone else killed, right?" he asked with a grin.

"Uh, yeah, right," she said with her head slightly lowered.

"No, Lisa. He's the first and hopefully the last. I try to give people chances, but he crossed me way too many times for any more chances. I didn't appreciate all of the disrespect and extortion threats all the time. If he needed money that bad then he needed to find a better job since I heard that he did work some shitty low-paying job. You don't try to extort money out of people just because you're broke."

"I agree. And tried to ruin my marriage on top of it."

"Well, I'm glad I was able to save it since that video has been deleted from his phone by my man and we don't believe there's any other copy of it."

She breathed a sigh of relief. "Thank goodness for that. But did you ever find out who set his phone up in your office?"

"Not yet, but if I do then that person is gonna learn their lesson the hard way."

She didn't like the sound of this. "Please don't have that person killed."

He laughed. "So, I'm ready to be repaid for my good deed," he said, clearly changing the subject.

She knew exactly what he'd meant. She walked over to him as he still sat in his favorite chair and bent down in front of him . . . and generously repaid him for saving her marriage.

. . .

Over an hour later, she arrived back home. Once again, she walked into a very dark house which was a direct reflection of the mood in it for a few days since her discovery, but unlike her, she had no proof of his cheating. They hadn't talked since.

She went into the family room and found the TV on and Greg once again sleeping on the couch. She just knew he would've at least called or texted her to see where she was all of this time even though they were mad at each other. It was as if he didn't care anymore.

She walked up the steps to their bedroom. *My marriage is in trouble,* she thought.

CHAPTER TWENTY-THREE

"She came in late last night. She didn't think I knew since I was sleeping on the couch. I've been sleeping there since she found the earring in my pants pocket. I haven't slept in our bed since," Greg said, as he sat in his office on his lunch break talking to Mitchell.

He shook his head. "Damn. I don't know what to say, man. All relationships are different, you know. So you think it's definitely Nigel she's cheating on you with?"

"I know it's Nigel, man, I just can't prove it. She's been acting like a different person since she met him. I don't know why she acts as if she has to talk to someone like him all of the time. There's nothing he can do for her that I can't do, and deep down inside she knows that."

"I don't see why so many women are talking about wanting to be his next wife since he's in the process of getting a divorce. I tell them all the time that a man like that isn't worth their time. He cares for no one but himself. And my wife has asked me did you have any proof of Lisa seeing him and I told her you didn't."

"No, I don't. I wish I had something because if I did then I told her that she's gonna be in big trouble."

"Now don't go doing anything crazy, man. No one is worth you getting into any trouble over, even your wife."

"I know, man. I'm just so upset about all of this. I just don't know how to keep her away from him. She's acting as if we're not even married by always talking about him and even having a meet-up with one of his half-siblings. I just wish she would concentrate on us and our marriage and us starting our family instead of wanting to be all up in other people's business."

"Sounds like she's really bored and lonely, Greg. Maybe the two of you should go on another vacation."

"I suggested that, but she doesn't want to. I know we've been all around the world more than once and she claims she's still bored and lonely. At this point I feel she's just too spoiled and selfish. I should suggest for her ass to get a job for real and see what she says, even though I suggested it to her once before."

He laughed. "I did that with my wife and recorded her reaction and as you and a whole lotta other people saw, it wasn't pretty. Then she threw in our kids as to the reason why she couldn't work outside the home. You know I only cheated on her once and she forgave me and we've been good ever since, but that's us."

"Yeah, that's you two. I wish Lisa and I were doing as well in our marriage as the two of you are doing in yours. I just want this to happen with her getting pregnant. I've waited now for ten years for this to happen. We just gotta work on being able to communicate again like we once did. Before she met Nigel I admit that I could see how bored and lonely she was, but what am I supposed to do? I need to work to continue to build for us especially since we're trying to have a child. I want my child to have a great legacy he or she can be proud of, and that starts by having a strong marriage. I don't want my child coming into this world with parents that are full of hostility and more hate than love for each other. What kind of shit is that?"

Mitchell shook his head. "Damn, man. Has it really gotten that bad between the two of you?"

He sighed. "I don't wanna say that it has, but it's definitely headed in that direction, but I'm gonna do what I can to get us back on the right track but she's gotta meet me halfway with it."

"And I know she will. Lisa's a great woman. I would've objected to you marrying her if I didn't think so. We all have problems, all of us. And the thing about problems is that they have solutions. I know the two of you will work out what y'all need to work out and will continue to build your lives together and it will be on a whole other level when you have your first child. I gotta feeling I'm gonna be hearing some good news real soon."

He smiled with a nod. "I really hope so, man."

They turned their attention to the TV:

"We have Breaking News. A man walking his dog found a body in the middle of the end of a deserted road. The police won't say how the man died or how he ended up where he ended up. No identification has been made on him as of yet. We'll be following this story and will keep you all updated as new information becomes available," the anchorman said.

Greg and Mitchell watched in horror as police surrounded the body of Lisa's blackmailer which now had a yellow tarp over it.

"Damn, that's fucked up," Mitchell said. "It was clear he was murdered. They're not gonna tell us that, though. I have a friend who works in Homicide so I'll call him and ask him more about it even though I'm really not supposed to since they just opened this case. You know I'm always intrigued with these types of cases."

"Yeah, I have to admit I'm curious as well. Let me know what you find out."

CHAPTER TWENTY-FOUR

Sharita sat in Lisa's kitchen as her mouth hung wide open after Lisa had told her what'd happened last night. "This is crazy, Lisa! What the hell?! I didn't know Nigel would have someone killed over you having an affair with him! Holy shit!"

"Well, I believe it was more about him protecting his money more than it was about protecting my marriage to Greg. He cares more about money than anything and works hard at making it and wants to keep it, of course. The last thing he wants to do is give it away to some broke blackmailer who's been harassing him online and everything for a long time. If I knew he was gonna do this, I wouldn't have gone to him for the money. I would've had to take the chance of Greg finding out. I feel Greg knows anyway about my cheating on him with Nigel like how I know he's cheating on me with some woman he probably works with. But neither of us have any proof of each other's infidelities."

"Well, now you can finally get back on track with your marriage since all of this is over with in terms of this blackmailer. Damn, that's a hard way to learn a lesson, but I guess when a person constantly threatens someone then they should know it's probably not gonna end well with them and in his case it didn't. Do you know who he is?"

"No, I have no idea. Nigel never told me. I don't even know the man's name who shot him; he's obviously someone who works for Nigel. Since it's all taken care of, I guess he feels that I don't have to know."

"Damn, Lisa. It seems like you're all caught up in some gangsta shit. This scares me. I think you really need to call off this affair with Nigel and work on your marriage with Greg. The more it seems like you see him, the more shit happens."

"Well, nothing is gonna happen anymore since what happen had. And by no means is Nigel the leader of a gang; never has been and never will be."

"I know he isn't. That was rhetorical. But he had someone killed, Lisa. *That's* serious. And he did it to protect you and your marriage to Greg, but now like you said, I feel he did it more to protect his money. And I know he didn't let you get away scot-free without repaying him, right?"

She lowered her head. "Yeah, you're right. I gave him some of the best head he's ever had. At least that's what he told me."

Sharita shook her head with a grin. "You've gotten way in over your head with him, Lisa. Please consider not seeing him anymore. You have been building a great future with Greg for well over ten years now. I feel the two of you starting your family is right around the corner. We're all excited for the two of you."

"I know all of you are. Greg and I have a lot to talk about. I know I let Nigel come between us, but not to a point where we're fighting every day about him. I'm just glad that he's never gonna find out that I cheated on him with him, but he still needs to admit to me that he's cheated on me. When he does that then we can get the counseling we need and move on in our marriage."

"Sounds good, Lisa."

They were interrupted by Breaking News:

"We have Breaking News on the story we brought you earlier about the man's body that was found in the middle of a deserted road by a man walking his dog early this morning. He's been identified as 29-year-old Pierce Tatum. Still at this hour there are no leads on any suspects in this case because Homicide has confirmed this to be a murder. Continue to stay with us for the latest updates on this case," the anchorman said.

Sharita looked at her. "So, that's his name. He doesn't sound familiar to me."

"Yeah, not to me, either. You know I also told you I had no idea what him nor what the man who shot him look like since they were completely covered up." She sighed. "Damn. I still can't believe I witnessed it! I couldn't even sleep last night," she said, and then poured herself another cup of coffee.

"I can't believe it, either. I thought you were kidding at first. I bet it felt like a movie, huh?"

"That's *exactly* what it felt like!"

She stared at her as she sipped her coffee.

"What?" Lisa asked.

"Are you planning on going to the cops with what you witnessed?"

"Are you fuckin' crazy, Sharita? Do you want Nigel to kill me?! Because I believe he probably will if I went to the cops about this. Remember, I have no idea who the man is who killed Pierce, and it was clear he was covered up because he was gonna do what he did and didn't want me to identify him. And we know Pierce was covered up because he didn't want me to identify him as well, but it was clear he didn't know he was being set up by Nigel and the killer. I feel that since the killer was covered up that Nigel doesn't trust me in the fact that I won't go to the cops. When I spoke to him after this happened last night, he didn't even mention anything about me going to the cops and to be honest, I didn't think about it that much, either. I guess I'm still so shocked over all of it."

"Yeah, it sounds like he didn't bring it up because he knows you never even thought about going to the cops."

"Yeah, I think so, too. I think he trusts me that I won't. I didn't have to tell him that I wasn't gonna go to the cops. I feel Pierce learned his lesson the hard way of extorting money and in the absolute worst way you can learn it in. I don't agree with him being killed over it, but he took the chance of that happening to him."

"Unfortunately, he did."

"Some people have to die to learn their life's lesson, and that's what unfortunately happened to Pierce. Like I said, I didn't want him to die over it and I can say with a clear conscience that I didn't know Nigel was gonna have him killed until it happened, and the driver said it was courtesy of the High-Nine-Figure Man. I knew instantly that they set him up to kill him all along. I just couldn't believe it. I'm afraid to fall asleep at night because I think I'm gonna have nightmares about it."

"Perfectly understandable, Lisa. But you know one thing's for sure, Pierce won't be bothering you or anyone else about trying to extort money out of them over shit that was none of his business."

"That's for sure."

CHAPTER TWENTY-FIVE

The scent of spaghetti and meatballs in marinara sauce with the finest of Italian spices overwhelmed the kitchen as Greg walked through the door from the garage. He found Lisa hard at work putting together the final preparations for dinner.

"Hi," he said with a smile.

"Hi," she replied as well with a genuine smile. "How was your day?"

"Great. Even more great now." He sat his work bag down. "What brought on all of this?"

"All of what, Greg? Me making dinner? You act as if I never make it."

"You haven't made it lately."

"Well, I'm making it now again as you can see. I'm doing what I should be doing as your wife. You know I always like for you to come home to a nice dinner."

He nodded with a smile as he stared at her. "Come here."

She walked over to him with a smile. They hugged and kissed.

"It feels good to have you back in my arms again, Lisa, it really does. I felt so alone these past few days."

"So have I, Greg. I just hate it when we fight and it's extended for long periods of time. I just don't like it when it's like this for us. We've been together for too long and we're trying to start our family. We need all of the positive energy we can get."

"I agree, Lisa, so we need to forget about every bad thing that's happened recently and put the focus back on us once again."

She smiled as they still held each other. "And I definitely agree with that."

They kissed once again.

"Let's eat this wonderful dinner you made for us in front of the TV tonight. What do you say?" he asked.

"Sure, that's fine. I actually prefer it. There's a new show coming on that I wanna watch."

"Is it gonna make me fall asleep?" he asked with a grin.

"Greg!" she said as she hit him. "I honestly don't know. *I* may end up falling asleep if I get bored with it!"

They laughed as they got their plates ready and walked into the family room. She was glad that they were finally talking to each other again and working on their marriage. She was also glad that her marriage was saved, and since she knew that it was, she would always be indebted to Nigel because of it.

During a commercial break from the show, the doorbell rang.

They looked at each other.

"Are you expecting anyone?" she asked.

"No. Are you?"

"I'm not expecting anyone, either, I'm just expecting some stuff I ordered, but I thought it was supposed to be here tomorrow. Maybe it did come a day early because sometimes it does."

They walked to the door.

He opened it while she stood beside him.

"Hello, folks. I'm Detective Reg Webber and this is Detective Kami Arnez, we're from Homicide. Are you Lisa Everett?"

Lisa felt herself go into a complete panic. "Yes," she said while her voice was visibly shaking.

"What is this about? What do you wanna talk to my wife about?" Greg asked.

"About the murder of Pierce Tatum, sir," Webber informed him.

Greg immediately turned and looked at Lisa.

"I don't know anything about it. I never knew Pierce," Lisa informed them.

"Can we come in to discuss this further?" Arnez asked.

Lisa looked at Greg as if she wanted him to decide whether or not they should enter their home.

"Yeah, come on in. We just got through eating dinner and were watching a boring show," Greg replied as he continued to stare at Lisa.

They walked in as Lisa felt her knees were about to buckle as Greg led them to the living room.

"Just make yourselves comfortable," Greg said, as Webber and Arnez sat down on the couch facing another couch which him and Lisa sat on. "Can I offer you both anything to drink?"

"No thanks, we're good," Webber replied.

Lisa was visibly shaking now. Greg kept staring at her since he noticed it, but refused to say a word.

"Um, I just don't understand why the two of you wanna talk to me about someone I didn't know," Lisa said as her voice shook.

"Well, we wouldn't be here if there wasn't a reason for it, Lisa," Webber informed her. "Where were you last night around 7:00pm?"

Greg looked at her for her answer.

"I was right here at home," she replied.

"Can you vouch for that, Mr. Everett?" Arnez asked.

Lisa looked at him.

Greg sighed. "You can call me Greg. And . . . no, I can't. I wasn't here yet myself. I was still finishing up at work."

Arnez wrote down what he'd said. "So your colleagues can verify that?"

"Absolutely they can," Greg informed her.

"Lisa, we don't wanna go around in circles with you. The reason why we are questioning you in the murder of Pierce Tatum is because he has some very interesting texts to you from his home computer," Webber informed her.

Lisa felt herself go into a full-blown panic. She knew about Pierce's killer taking his phone, but didn't even think about the fact that his texts to her were also connected to his home computer. "That doesn't mean I had him killed!"

"So you're admitting that you had an exchange of texts with Pierce in the past few days?" Arnez asked.

Greg gave her a very daunting glare as he waited for her answer.

"Yes, I did," she confessed with her head lowered. "This guy was known for blackmailing people. He claimed he had proof that I was cheating on my husband when he didn't!"

"But he did," Webber informed her.

"WHAT?!" Greg asked as he jumped up and stared down at Lisa. "So it's true, huh? You are fucking Nigel Foreman!"

"And you're fucking some bitch you work with!" Lisa yelled back.

"Okay, calm down, you two. We don't wanna have to arrest the two of you for being disorderly. Greg, I know this is your house but can you sit over there, please? I think it would be better right now," Webber said.

Greg nodded in agreement and sat in a chair away from Lisa as he still glared at her.

"Well, since Nigel Foreman was brought up, he was questioned as well just so you know, Lisa. How well do you know him?" Arnez asked.

"Not that well. We've only known each other for a short period of time," she replied.

"And I told her to stay away from him," Greg informed them.

Webber and Arnez looked at Lisa.

"I just don't see any harm in talking to him. I consider him a friend," Lisa tried to explain. "He acts as if he doesn't want me having any male friends."

"Yeah, just like how you don't want me having any female friends," Greg replied.

"I don't care if you have female friends—"

"As long as they don't look better than you," Greg interrupted her.

"Okay, you two. We don't mean to cause a fight between the two of you, we're just trying to get some information that'll eventually lead us to a suspect for this murder we're trying to solve," Webber said.

"And I don't know anything about it. I told you all what I know. I didn't know Pierce at all. Yes, I do know Nigel, though. He didn't tell me anything about Pierce so I had no idea that he knew of him," Lisa said.

"But how did you know he was a blackmailer? Because, you know, Nigel told us the same thing about him being a blackmailer," Arnez informed her.

Greg gave her another very daunting glare.

"Because of what he was trying to do to me, that's why! What would you call someone who texts you out of nowhere and claim they have something on you and then demand a ridiculous amount of money to make it go away or else they'll expose it for the world to see? Huh? They're either a blackmailer or an extortionist, take your pick because they both mean the same thing!"

Webber and Arnez looked at each other.

"Funny how you brought up the money part, Lisa, because that part was never reported to the media," Arnez informed her.

"Lisa, what the fuck is going on here? You better start talking more and you better start talking right now!" Greg demanded.

"Calm down, Greg. This is why we're here so we can see what she knows about this," Webber said.

"I know *nothing* about this!" Lisa said as tears welled up in her eyes. "If you all think I had something to do with this then you're wrong! That man tried to extort money out of me, money I don't have!"

"But Nigel Foreman has it," Webber said.

"I don't think I can hear any more of this," Greg said.

"You're free to leave if you wish, Greg, since you're not the one we're here to question," Arnez informed him.

Lisa looked at him as tears streamed from her eyes.

"No, I think I'll stay. As much as I don't wanna hear this I feel I have to. I'm finding out shit that I don't think I would've ever found out," he said as he still kept his daunting glare on Lisa.

"According to these documents, Nigel Foreman has a personal net worth of over $875 million dollars. Almost at billionaire status. So you going to him to get this amount would've been perfect for you to do, right?"

"I didn't go to Nigel to get any money!" she lied.

"Well, we can't prove that you did, but we can prove that Nigel withdrew $100,000 in cash from one of his many personal accounts, and the money was never put back into this particular account nor into any of his other accounts. The money was never found on Pierce, either, and why would a large amount like that be found on him if he was murdered? Clearly someone promised to give him that money and then set him up to be killed so they wouldn't have to give it to him after all," Webber said.

Greg continued to glare at Lisa.

"Well, it wasn't me! *I swear* it wasn't! I didn't have anything to do with setting anyone up to be murdered because of me having an affair with Nigel!"

"Glad to see you finally admit it," Greg said.

She gasped! Not realizing what she'd said. Webber and Arnez stared at her, and Webber wrote down what she'd finally admitted to.

Greg shook his head. "If you had that man killed because you didn't want me knowing that you were fucking Nigel, then you know what's gonna happen. I don't care what he tried to extort out of you, if you set him up to be murdered then it's over between us."

"I didn't set him up to be murdered, Greg! I didn't! Why don't you believe me?! I DIDN'T!!!" she screamed.

"Calm down, Lisa. We're not accusing you of setting Pierce up to be murdered, okay? We're just trying to find out what happened. There's no proof you got any money from Nigel to pay Pierce and then set him up to be murdered so you wouldn't have to pay him after all, nor is there any proof that Nigel set him up to have him murdered so he wouldn't have to pay him. Nigel could've done anything with that $100,000—he told us he withdraws money in that amount often, but we didn't see any evidence of it so that's what made us suspicious.

"However, you can't deny the fact that these texts between you and Pierce don't exist with him trying to extort $100,000 out of you or else he was gonna expose the affair you were having with Nigel. But you're right, we have no proof of what happened between when these texts were exchanged up to the time of him being killed. So, since we don't have anything criminal to charge you with, then we'll conclude this interview," Webber said.

Lisa felt a big wave of relief wash over her. "Thank you."

"Thank you for talking with us," Webber and Arnez said.

Minutes after Greg showed them out, he walked past her towards the stairs.

"Greg, we need to talk about this some more."

He sighed. "There's nothing else to talk about, Lisa, because all you're gonna do is lie to me like what you did to those cops. You let yourself get way in too deep with Nigel and now you almost had a murder charge on you because of it. You may have fooled those cops, but you didn't fool me. Either you really did have Pierce set up to be murdered, or you know that Nigel did and didn't wanna tell them because you're trying to protect a man that doesn't give a shit about you or anyone but himself. Only you know all of the real answers to what I'm saying, Lisa, and only you will have to be the one to tell the truth about it all because the truth *can't* and *won't* stay a secret forever. But whatever the truth is, I hope you learn your lesson from it."

CHAPTER TWENTY-SIX

"HE'S GONNA DIVORCE ME, I CAN FEEL IT," LISA SAID IN A PANIC AS SHE paced back and forth in the kitchen of Chassy's home.

"What makes you think that, Lisa? I just don't think he is. You were telling the truth that you had nothing to do with setting up Pierce to be murdered—that was all Nigel. I have to agree and have always agreed with Greg about the fact that you just need to stay away from Nigel. Think about it, he really didn't save your marriage because he had Pierce killed instead of you giving him the money like how you told me it was all originally planned. I knew when you told me you were getting the money from Nigel, I can't lie, I was surprised. But then again I thought about the fact that there was no way someone like him was gonna part with $100,000 to give to a blackmailer over a woman he's having an affair with so she can save her marriage—no offense."

"None taken. Seriously. I had to come to the conclusion that that is what he was thinking all along even though he never flat-out told me. I just know, you know?"

"Yeah, I know, Lisa. And I want you to know something as well. Nigel is still legally married. There hasn't been anything about his divorce being finalized yet. Everyone knows it's gonna happen, but it hasn't happened yet. Like I said, he's just someone most women should stay away from. Yeah, I had a crush on him and everything, but as you see the more you started to tell me about him, all that shit went out the door. He just doesn't seem like a good person, and now he's really not a good person since he had Pierce murdered just so you wouldn't have to pay him with Nigel's money after all, and you were right in the middle of it!"

"I know, Chassy. I still can't believe it. Like I said, I was *never, ever* afraid before in my life more than I was standing out in the middle of a dead-end deserted road out in the middle of nowhere with a brief-case that had $100,000 in cash in it. When I saw there wasn't just one man but two who got out the car, I instantly panicked and was gonna drop the briefcase and get into my car and screech off. Just standing there waiting for the exchange to happen and then something happened that I never even thought would happen made me realize just how much of a mess I'd gotten into with Nigel."

"Well, now you'll be officially out of this mess if you just tell the cops the truth about what really happened."

"I can't snitch on Nigel, Chassy. Do you want him to kill me?"

"Do you want him to get away with murder?"

Lisa sighed as she stared out the patio doors.

"Because if you don't tell the cops the truth, Lisa, that's what's gonna happen. I know Pierce was a blackmailer, but he didn't deserve to die over it. Nigel is the type of man who thinks the rules just don't apply to him. Just because he didn't pull the trigger doesn't mean he didn't kill him. He clearly ordered the hit and you witnessed it, and I can't even put it into words how horrible that is because no one should witness someone being unexpectedly executed right in from of them."

"Yeah, it was unexpected and it was definitely an execution, no doubt about it. I even thought for a second that the killer was gonna kill me for witnessing it."

Chassy shook her head. "Damn, I'm glad he didn't. But if this doesn't get you to leave Nigel alone, Lisa, then I don't know what will."

"Well, I feel like now I have to keep talking to him because I'm not gonna lie, I'm afraid that if I abruptly stop then he's gonna think I'm up to something; like I am planning on going to the cops to tell them the truth about what'd happened, but I can't do that without proof."

"In that case, Lisa, then maybe you should keep talking to him so you can get the proof you need. It's very easy to get people on video confessing."

"My only thing, Chassy, is that we did talk about it and he pretty much warned me about not saying anything to anyone about it. He gave me a look that he'd never given me before and I knew that was a warning look because he was well aware of what I'd witnessed."

"It scares me all the time to think about the fact that every time you see Nigel that something bad could possibly happen."

"Everything bad that's happened when it comes to me and Nigel has already happened. Yeah, I can't say anymore that he officially saved my marriage because he had the blackmailer killed and the money is back with him. When I went over to his house to talk to him just a few hours after it'd happened, I saw the briefcase sitting on the floor with blood spatter on it since it was a tan color one. I almost threw up. It showed me that the killer really did give all the money back to him. I mean, that briefcase was very clean in my hands when I left his house with it and full of cash, and then hours later it was right back at his house full of cash but with blood spatter all over it. And he was talking to me as if it was just his work brief-case that sat there all the time. I couldn't believe it."

"Yeah, I can't believe you're telling me all of this. It's one of those stories you wanna tell everyone but you know you're sworn to secrecy about?"

"Exactly, Chassy, because I know I am. I will always carry this guilt with me about knowing what I know. I know Greg knows I know a lot more than what I told those cops, but I just can't get any more deeply involved in this than I already am. I need to move on from it and with my marriage to Greg. And just to think I made him a nice dinner and we watched a show while eating and those cops came knocking at our door during a commercial break. It's like I couldn't believe they were standing there when Greg opened the door. I was so shocked that I didn't know why they were there at first, then it hit me. I've never had cops question me about anything."

"And this all started because of your involvement with Nigel, Lisa. You see how you've never had cops show up at your door with anything concerning Greg. Nigel is trash—the whole Foreman family is—and now he's a murderer from what you've told me, and murderers don't always have to physically commit an actual murder as anyone with sense knows."

"Oh, I definitely know that, Chassy. I just have to be careful because I know he's gonna wanna keep seeing me as his way of keeping his eye on me because I know he doesn't completely trust me that I won't go to the cops. Well, I didn't have to go to the cops, they came to me."

"And if you don't want them to keep coming to you then you really need to tell them the truth. Fuck Nigel. His ass and the man who killed Pierce need to be in prison. Nigel isn't above anything, Lisa. Please remember that."

"I know. No one is."

CHAPTER TWENTY-SEVEN

"I tried to get here as fast as I could, man. What's up? What's going on?" Greg asked, as he sat down in a chair in front of Mitchell's desk where he worked.

Mitchell shook his head. "Damn, man."

"What?" Greg asked again. "Don't hold me in suspense, man. What is it?"

He sighed. "You know I told you I know someone in Homicide, right?"

Greg shook his head as he lowered it. "Just say what you gotta say, man."

"Now this can't be confirmed, but I need for you to take a look at something that my man found while working the Pierce Tatum crime scene." He gave his phone to him.

Greg took it from him and looked at it. He let out a long, loud sigh and shoved it back to him.

Mitchell kept staring at him. "What's up, man? Do you recognize it? Because my man can get in a hell of a lot of trouble if someone finds out that he took this item from the crime scene and it's not on record. It can't be proven that it's a part of the crime scene and could be anyone's. But it was near the crime scene so more than likely it has something to do with it."

"It has everything to do with it," Greg confirmed. "That's a charm from a charm bracelet I bought Lisa for her birthday a few years back. She's never taken that bracelet off until recently. I notice she hasn't worn it for several days, but I haven't said anything. The bracelet has so many charms on it that I don't even think she knows this one is missing from it. It's real gold. All the charms and the bracelet are. Some of the charms have real diamonds on them and this one was one of them." He slammed his fist down on his desk!

Mitchell jumped back in his seat. "Try to calm down, man. You need to talk to her about this once again. It's clear she was there and was lying to you and the cops about something."

Greg cupped his hands over his head as he sat back in his chair. "I didn't wanna believe that she was actually there, man, I really didn't. I can't believe this shit!" He got up out of his chair and paced around the office. "This Nigel motherfucker really fucked her up, he really did. It's like she's doing shit that she never used to do, and it started with her cheating on me with him. Now I see proof that she was actually there; *actually there* at the crime scene! This is on a whole other level now, Mitch. I don't know what I'm gonna do about this or her."

"Look, man, don't go doing anything crazy, okay? I mean it. Now that it's been confirmed that the item found is hers, I want you to stay calm. Do you want me to go with you to talk to her?"

"No, man. I have to do this by myself. It's my problem, not anyone else's."

Greg busted through the front door of their home. "LISA! LISA!" he roared while he stomped through the house. "LISA! WHERE THE FUCK ARE YOU?! WE NEED TO TALK AND WE NEED TO TALK RIGHT NOW!"

He checked the entire house. She wasn't here. He took a few deep breaths, grabbed a bottle of beer out of the refrigerator, and sat down at the kitchen island counter. He then got up and went upstairs to their bedroom and searched through one of her larger jewelry boxes . . . and found the gold charm bracelet buried deep within it. He took out his phone and looked at the picture Mitchell had sent to him with the missing charm. He examined the bracelet carefully.

Confirmed.

The sparkling diamond flower charm was in fact missing. He sighed as he shook his head and walked out of the bedroom and back downstairs with the bracelet in his hand.

Lisa walked through the door over an hour later with a few bags of groceries in her hands . . . to Greg sitting at the kitchen island counter. "Greg, what's wrong? You're home early."

He pulled out the charm bracelet. "How come you haven't been wearing your bracelet, Lisa? You haven't taken it off since I gave it to you a few years ago."

"I . . . just wanted to give it a break, that's all. I got a lot of beautiful jewelry so I just wanted to rotate some pieces once again like I was doing before you got me the bracelet."

"It's not because a charm is missing from it, is it?"

She felt herself going into a panic. "There are no charms missing, Greg."

"Don't even start fuckin' lying to me, Lisa. You need to sit down and shut the fuck up right now. I know all about it so don't try to lie to me." He shoved the bracelet over to her. "See for yourself."

She examined the bracelet. "Wow, I didn't even notice, Greg, I swear I didn't."

"Don't lie to me!" he yelled.

"Why are you yelling?"

"Because you're fuckin' lying, that's why! And you lied to those cops that were here, too! What the fuck has gotten into you, Lisa?

You've been really fucked up since you got yourself involved with that Nigel motherfucker. I don't even know who the fuck you are anymore!"

Her eyes welled up with tears. "I'm still the same person, Greg. I haven't changed since I met Nigel. I don't see how this bracelet has anything to do with him. It's not like he's the one who gave it to me, and for the record he's never given me anything."

"Yeah, he better not have because I'll knock his fuckin' head off if he did."

"Come on, Greg. Stop it, okay? I'm tired of us always arguing. Did you wanna help me with dinner tonight since you're home early? You usually do when you are."

"Lisa, what kind of a fuckin' fool do you take me for? Don't try to change the fuckin' subject—*fuck* dinner!" He shoved his phone to her with the picture of the charm on it as it laid on the ground of the deserted road.

She kept staring at it. She knew she couldn't deny this anymore that it was in fact the charm missing from her bracelet.

He snatched the bracelet as it sat in front of her. "Hmmm, first the charm was there and now it's not. And that's probably one of the most expensive ones on this overpriced gaudy thing," he said as he examined it once again.

Tears began to stream down from her eyes. "I don't wanna go to prison, Greg. I did all of this for you. I wanted to save our marriage. If Nigel didn't care about me and my marriage to you he wouldn't have given me the money to give to Pierce."

"But Pierce never got the money, now did he? I think any idiot knows that he was killed by one of Nigel's little cronies, right? Sounds like the perfect setup."

"And I didn't set him up to be killed, Greg! I told those cops the truth!"

"You know that's the only part of the story I believe, Lisa. But Nigel didn't give a shit about saving your marriage to me. He gave you money to give to a guy and then had him killed so he wouldn't have to pay him after all. Since I love you, I'm not gonna say anything about you being there at the scene since I believe you didn't know it was a setup and you went there with the intentions you told me you went there for. But this is what happens when you get yourself involved with a man who you had no business getting involved with; it never turns out well. You need to promise me from here on out that you will leave that motherfucker alone. Can you promise me that? Because you could've gotten killed that night."

"I know, Greg. And I'm sorry. I thought I was gonna be killed for a second when he shot him—and no, I have no idea who the guy is who shot him because not only was Pierce covered up, but his killer was as well. It was the most horrible thing I've ever witnessed. I don't *ever* wanna witness anything like that in my life ever again!" she said, and broke down and cried.

He embraced her. "I know, Lisa. But this is what happens when shit goes too far and you get involved with people you have no business getting involved with. I know you did it for us, but you could've been killed as well, like I said, because anything can pop off in situations like that. I had no idea what I would take to my grave, but now I know your involvement in this is probably what it's gonna be."

"I said the same thing when I came home that night after witnessing this."

"But you're not lying about not knowing who killed Pierce?"

"No, I have no idea who he is. I never see too many of Nigel's friends or people who work for him, plus, like I said, he was completely covered up."

He nodded. "Okay, I believe you."

"Um, is there any way I can get my charm back?"

"I don't see why not. Mitch told me that the cop who sent him the picture said that no one knows he took it from the scene. Remember, they're friends and that's the only reason why he did this is because Mitch told him you knew Nigel. He told Mitch he didn't know whether or not it was part of the crime scene or not, so if I can get it back from him, Lisa, we're gonna have to have him over for dinner more than once because Mitch told me he loves to eat."

She chuckled. "That won't be a problem at all. I have a lot to thank him for."

CHAPTER TWENTY-EIGHT

"So, you didn't know it was missing, huh?" Nigel said, as he examined Lisa's charm bracelet himself. "This is a nice bracelet, and this charm that was missing is one of the best ones on here."

"It is. It's actually my favorite charm. When I saw that it was missing I went into a panic. I didn't notice it until the next day. I knew I couldn't go back to the crime scene to get it."

"It's good that you didn't because it's only a charm and very well could not have been a part of the crime scene. That's great that the cop gave it to your husband's best friend to give to him to give back to you. I'm gonna have to put that cop on my payroll. Big shout out to your husband for not saying anything about you being there as well. He knew you meant well and had nothing to do with killing that motherfucker."

"And he said he believes me. He said he's gonna take it to his grave knowing that I was there at the scene because he knew I lied to the cops about not being there and all. I'm just glad that I was able to get my charm back on my bracelet."

"And I was glad to get my money back," he said with a smile. "If that motherfucker thought he was gonna go the roundabout way of getting money from me then he found out the hard way and learned his lesson from it, and that's a hell of a way to learn a lesson."

"Yeah, the deadly way is the worst way you can learn it; most definitely is." She sat back on his couch. "You know, sometimes I wonder if this is really it."

"If what is really it, Lisa?" he asked with a smile.

She sighed. "I have to be honest with you, Nigel."

"That's the only way I want you to be with me."

"Greg said he didn't want me to ever see you again, especially now since this happened. I still can't trust the fact that he won't go to the cops because he knows what happened and he knows I was there and that you had everything to do with it."

"He can't prove a damn thing if he does go to them."

"Yeah, I know he can't, but I still can't and won't have the comfort that he won't, you know. I just feel that every time we get into another fight he's gonna bring this shit up. He said that you turned me into a different person."

"Have I?" he asked as he stared at her.

"No, I don't think you have, and I told him that. I'm the same Lisa everyone knows. It's just that I didn't know that everything that was gonna happen between us was gonna happen."

"Yeah, well, no one knew. That's life, though. We didn't know we were gonna see each other at the bakery shop the day that we met, right?"

"Yeah, you're right."

"So, you know, just think if you didn't go there or if I didn't go there on that day and at that time we would've never met, right?"

"Right."

"Things happen for a reason, Lisa, and it's not always a bad thing. Despite what has happened since we met, I don't regret meeting you. Do you regret meeting me?"

"Absolutely not," she replied. "I always tell Greg I just feel that there's no harm in me still talking to you. Yes, what happened that night of the murder I didn't expect, but Pierce was gonna get it from someone for all of his blackmailing, and he got it from you."

"He actually got it from my man."

She wasn't gonna argue with him knowing that he ordered the hit. "Yeah, he did."

"Since this is all behind us now, let's make this a new beginning in our relationship, Lisa."

"I wasn't aware that we were in a relationship."

"Well, not the way you think we are, but I think now we can build on making things better from here on out if you want; if your husband will let you."

"I'm a grown woman. He can't tell me what to do. I enjoy your company and you enjoy mine. I don't see anything wrong with us still talking to each other like the way we are now. Besides, I'm sure he's doing a whole lotta talking to more women as well as other things that he doesn't wanna admit to me that he's doing. You know he *still* hasn't admitted to me that he's cheated on me?"

"Doesn't surprise me, Lisa. The surprise would've been if he *wasn't* cheating on you."

She smirked. "Yeah, I know. I just don't know how long this cheating is gonna go on with him if he is doing it. I admitted to only cheating on him with you and it's not like we have sex all the time when we see each other. I know what we did was wrong and at least I'm woman enough to admit it."

"Well, it's too bad you're not single so you don't have to worry about what your man does."

"If he was my boyfriend I would still worry about it because he did cheat on me a lot before we got married even though he tried to deny it; I was hesitate to marry him because of it. And I never cheated on him until I met you. I just don't think this is gonna stop."

"That's why Aisha and I are in the process of getting a divorce. I just wanted to be free to do whatever the hell I want and not be nagged all the time about any and everything. I took it for as long as I could."

"Sometimes divorce is the best option and in your case it was. I feel that I got married a little too young, yes, I thought being married at twenty-six was too young. I should've waited at least four more years or something before I did, but he wanted to do it then since he was thirty, and he was my boyfriend since my freshman year in high school and he was a senior, so I did it."

"But you don't seem happy about your decision to marry young."

"I'm not a hundred percent happy, I'll admit that. But what's done is done with it. We've been officially married for ten years and I have to admit I don't think no other man would've given me the kind of lifestyle that Greg has."

"Are you sure about that?"

She stared at him. "Well, no. You're right. I can't say for sure. I'm only assuming, I guess." She sighed. "You know, sometimes I wish I met you when I was single, but I feel like I haven't been single since the eighth grade."

"You're only not single if you're married."

"Yeah, a lot of people say that, but even more don't believe it. I know I can't go back now, but I feel that I would've at least had more options than Greg and he would've had more options than me. It's like we didn't even give each other a chance to see who else was out there who could've been right for each of us. I've talked to him about it and he says he does regret that we didn't at least go our separate ways to explore other options, especially with us being four years apart. But he always says that we never did it because we were meant to be together all along so that's why everything happened the way it did."

"Sounds about right, Lisa. And I feel if you were truly unhappy then you wouldn't have wanted to save your marriage to him, either, and all the shit that's happened in the past days would've never happened."

"Yeah, you're right about that. I would've never went that far."

"Sometimes our marriages are tested on what we will do or what we won't do to save them. And you were willing to give a large amount of money to a stranger to save yours, and you came to me to get it. I know how hard that was for you to do."

"Harder than you'll ever know. But yeah, I was willing to save it and did what I had to do because I thought it was worth saving."

"I know you did. But as you know, I didn't think mine was worth saving at all. I don't care what Aisha does from here on out. She just better take care of my kids when they're not with me and not have a man staying with her because I'm not gonna have him living up in the lap of luxury all in a house that I've paid for and all the while using her and disrespecting my kids."

"Yeah, I wouldn't tolerate that either if I had kids."

"But enough about her. She knows any woman can replace her now and she has finally seen that as a reality. She doesn't know that I don't wanna get remarried and I have her to thank for that."

"But why not? Not all women are like her; and was she really that bad?"

"The worst," he replied, and took another sip of his drink. "But I know there's a better woman out there for me because like I've told you a lot, Lisa, I can give a woman the world. Aisha took every damn thing I gave her for granted. I even think she takes our kids for granted. Entitled-ass bitch. I don't want my next woman to be like that, not at all."

"Well, Nigel, you can have any woman you want, I think you know that."

"Yeah, I know," he said with a grin. "But that doesn't mean I want them."

"I know you have standards."

"That's right," he replied and took a sip of his drink. "This time a woman has to show me what she's willing to do for me in order for me to make her mine. Aisha just got lucky that we were together for years and got pregnant with our first child because that's the only reason why I married her. It's not gonna be like that this time around. Like I said, me and the world for my new girl is hers if she can show me what she can do for me. I can't wait."

They continued to stare at each other as they took another sip of their drinks.

CHAPTER TWENTY-NINE

"Greg?" Lisa said, as she walked upstairs to their bedroom. She noticed that it was pitch black in the hall. She turned on the lights and noticed their bedroom door closed. She opened it up to *him having sex with another woman*!

The woman jumped off of him as if he was on fire!

"YOU SON OF A BITCH!!" Lisa screamed, and grabbed a vase of flowers he'd given her and threw it directly at him!

It missed his head by inches and smashed into the wall!

"Lisa! Lisa, stop! Okay, stop!" he pleaded while the woman quickly put on her clothes as Lisa charged at her and tackled her to the ground!

"What the fuck are you doing fucking my husband, bitch?!" she yelled as she still had a good hold on her.

"Let go of me!" the woman pleaded as she tried to get out of Lisa's strong hold on her.

"Let go of her, Lisa, so she can go! Let go!" Greg said as he tried to get her off of her.

But Lisa was a lot stronger than she looked. She held on to the woman as hard and tight as she could, but her grip suddenly slipped and the woman was finally able to get out of her hold while she choked and tried to catch her breath, but Lisa got back up and kicked her in her ass and made her fall back to the ground!

"LISA! STOP, OKAY?! STOP!" Greg yelled as he finally had a strong hold on her.

The woman got back up and finally managed to gather up her things and quickly left the house.

They watched from their bedroom window as she staggered across the street, got into her car, and left.

"Yeah, clever. She parks across the street so it appeared as if she was at our neighbor's house since their driveway has cars in it. And, yeah, I thought she was at their house. There's plenty of space to park in front of our house and even in our driveway since both of our cars are in the garage," Lisa said.

Greg sighed. "We need to talk about this, Lisa."

"About what, Greg? About the proof that I finally have of you cheating on me? So, did you give her back her earring because I know that's her, right?"

He sighed. "Yeah, that's her."

"And you had the *nerve* to bring her in our house and fuck her in our bed, Greg? What the fuck is wrong with you? She was in *our bed*, Greg! *Our bed*! This bed is only for us to sleep in and make love in! This bed is only for our future children to be in with us when they can't sleep because they're sick or having nightmares! How the fuck can you do this, Greg?!"

"I fucked up, Lisa. I'm not perfect. We have to look past this. Now we both have proof that we cheated on each other, so we have to work through this. There was a reason why you caught me, and it serves me right that you did. This shows both of us that this is not a perfect marriage because no marriage is. We both disrespected our vows and it's up to us to once again to respect them; respect each other. I love you and only you, Lisa, you know that."

Tears streamed from her eyes. "I know, Greg. And I love you, too. I never expected our marriage to be perfect, but I admit I never thought both of us would cheat on each other, but it happened, and I don't want it to ever happen again."

"That's why we need to work on us, Lisa, so it won't happen again. Neither one of us are perfect, and now we can say since we have proof that we cheated on each other that we learned our lesson from it. I know I've learned mine. Have you learned yours?"

"Of course, Greg."

He came over to her and embraced her. "You're the only one I'll ever love."

"Same here," she said as she continued to cry. "But I want a brand-new bed with new covers and sheets and pillows and everything."

He laughed while they still embraced. "You got it."

Lisa and Greg stared at each other while they laid on opposite ends of their large curved family room sofa with their separate covers over them, with the only light coming from the TV.

"How did it get to this point, Greg? Where we're sleeping on the sofa not because we fell asleep during a boring movie, but because I don't wanna sleep in our bed because another woman was in it."

He sighed as he now stared up at the ceiling. "I know, Lisa. But like I said earlier, we both admitted to doing wrong, now it's time to move on. If we keep bringing this up and fighting about it then we're not gonna get anywhere. We owe each other that much. We hit a bad road in our marriage and now we gotta get back on the right one, the one we were on all along. No one can do it but us, don't you agree?"

Silence.

"Lisa?" he said, and looked at her.

She was sound asleep.

CHAPTER THIRTY

"Wow, this is a beautiful private plane, Nigel. It's amazing that you own this. We need more black people like you owning stuff like this," Lisa said, as she sat across from him in the back of the plane as Michael Jackson's "I Can't Help It" played softly through the speakers.

He smiled back at her while wearing a black suit, white shirt, and a black tie. He'd just gotten back from a business trip. "Yeah, I agree, Lisa. Not too many of our people own stuff like this. It's better to own things than rent them, lease them, you name it. This is what old money and new money along with decades of hard work looks like. I feel my family has come a long way, but we still have a long way to go. I wanna see more black families live like this."

"So do I," she said with a smile.

He returned the smile as he stared at her. "So, what brings you here? You said you had something important to tell me."

She sighed as she stared at the floor. "Yeah, I do. I finally have proof that Greg cheated on me. I caught him a few days ago in our bed with another woman."

"Doesn't surprise me, Lisa. Men just can't be faithful to women; I know that for a fact because I speak from experience. I think it's in a lot of our DNA."

"Yeah, I think it is, too. But you know, I can't talk. I cheated on him but *I swear* I only cheated on him with you. I just think he's done this more than I know, I just finally caught him this time."

"I hate to say this, Lisa, but you're probably right. I cheated on Aisha more times than I ever wanna admit that I did, I can't lie. The four kids by the three different women I had were a very tiny fraction of the number of women I cheated on her with overall. Those were just the ones that I ended up stupidly getting pregnant. But yeah, if a man has a chance to cheat then he's gonna cheat, Lisa, and it doesn't matter how beautiful you are and how much of a great wife you are; doesn't matter. When the opportunity is there, we take it without a second thought."

"Yeah, that's pretty damn obvious."

"So, the two of you are trying to work it out, huh?"

She sighed. "Yeah, we are. We were both wrong and we said we're willing to work on our marriage and to get it back on the right track."

"How come you don't seem so happy about it?"

"I'm happy, I just don't want it to fail. I'm just tired of all of what's been going on with us, and there's no guarantee that he's not gonna cheat on me again."

"He's gonna do it again like how you're gonna do it again. Hate to be blunt, but it's true."

"And I need to hear the truth."

"Well, that's why I set myself free from marriage. I couldn't deal with that shit anymore. It was never for me. I don't feel a woman needs to be married to me to live the way she wants to live. Every woman who is a good woman should have the chance at living the life she's always wanted to live, and I'm one of the very few men in this world that can provide her with that, especially with me being a black man. I never thought I'd say this and say it soon at that, but I'm getting kinda lonely myself because I haven't found any childless, unmarried women that fits what I'm looking for to share my lifestyle with, but I know she's out there. I've been with a ton of women since Aisha and I announced our divorce, but I haven't found anyone I want with me the majority of the time."

"Whoever gets you next is gonna be a very lucky woman."

He smiled as he stared at her. "More than she'll ever know."

CHAPTER THIRTY-ONE

Three firm knocks rattled the outside door of Greg's office.

"Come in," Greg said.

A person he'd never seen before appeared before him. "Dr. Greg Everett?"

"Yes?" he replied.

"These are for you," the man said, and turned and left.

"Thank you," he replied, and looked at what was handed to him. "WHAT?!"

Divorce papers.

Greg stormed through the front door of his home still in his scrubs since he was on his lunch break armed with the divorce papers he was served with at his place of work. "LISA! LISA! WHERE THE FUCK ARE YOU?!" He found her sitting at the kitchen island counter looking at her phone. "Lisa, *why* are you doing this? *Why*? This isn't right! You *can't* throw away ten years of marriage like this! Look what I've built for us?"

She sighed as she put down her phone. "Yeah, it's always what you've built for us, as if I had nothing to do with anything but shop-ping and sitting in this home watching TV and gossiping in person, online, and on the phone!"

"That's not what I meant, Lisa, and you know it. You have no grounds to do this!"

"Yeah, Greg, I think I have the perfect grounds to do this on. You know damn well you're never gonna stop cheating on me even after me catching you, and I can't say that I won't ever do it again to you. It's clear that we're just not in love with each other anymore."

He sighed as the papers hung by his side. "That's ridiculous, Lisa. Yeah, I fucked up just like how you fucked up. And I won't be cheating on you with her anymore because her husband plays professional sports and he got traded so they're moving this week. You know damn well we're still in love with each other. People just don't fall out of love with each other overnight, so can you call this shit off?"

Tears welled up in her eyes. "Why, Greg? It's clear that we've grown apart. Like I've said before and we both know, we've both cheated on each other so what makes us think we won't do it again? Because we promised each other we won't? This marriage has been in trouble for a while, so we might as well just call it what it is."

He shook his head. "I know *exactly* where you took a wrong turn at in our marriage, Lisa, and I'm not even gonna mention what turn you took because you know it all too well. But if you think the grass is greener over there then go. I'm not gonna hold you back, but I'm also not gonna hold out hope that you'll reconsider this, either. Only you know why you're really doing this, and you can give all of the excuses about us and our cheating on each other and our marriage and what the fuck ever. If you want out that bad then you can get the fuck out. I'm not gonna beg you to stay. You'll hear from my lawyer. Oh, and get the fuck out of this house as well. Take whatever you need for right now and I'll have the rest of your things sent to you. I don't wanna see you here when I get home later. You don't live here anymore."

CHAPTER THIRTY-TWO

"Never did I ever imagine that you would file for divorce from Greg, Lisa. This seems so surreal to me. Please tell me this is a joke," Sharita said.

"No, it's not a joke," Lisa confirmed, as she, along with Chassy, sat at the kitchen table in a house her parents owned that had yet to be rented. It was a single-story home and very small in size and didn't have half the space she was used to when she lived with Greg.

"I'm speechless. Just speechless. Never ever did it ever cross my mind that the two of you would be getting a divorce," Chassy said.

"And it didn't cross mine at all as well," Sharita said. "And you went through all of that gangsta shit to save your marriage only to divorce him? What is wrong with you, Lisa?"

"Greg was never gonna stop cheating on me, I don't care what he says. I just wasn't overall happy anymore, and it took me to really start talking to Nigel and accept the reality that Greg really did cheat on me like what I did to him to realize that we shouldn't be together after all. And I also believe that us not having a child was a sign that we shouldn't be together anymore because if it hasn't happened after ten years it was never gonna happen."

Sharita shook her head. "Not necessarily, Lisa. The two of you having a child could've still happened after ten years, it's happened for a lot of married couples after that time and sometimes even later than that. I just don't think it was right for you to divorce Greg. How do you know Nigel is really gonna want you now that you did?"

Chassy looked at Lisa for her answer.

"This isn't about Nigel, this is about my happiness and I wasn't happy anymore. I don't need everyone coming down on me for what I did. You all thought it was so great with Greg, but as you all see now it wasn't as great as you all thought it was. We cheated on each other because it was clear we were no longer happy with each other. We were just becoming more and more distant as well. We just needed to call it what it is—over."

Sharita and Chassy looked at each other.

"Well, you're right that we have no idea about everything that went on in your marriage to Greg, Lisa, but it's clear that something went horribly wrong in these past several weeks, and I'm gonna be honest with you—I think Nigel had a lot if not everything to do with it, but only you know if he did. You know we love you and we're your best friends, and we just don't wanna see you make a mistake like this. You and Greg had everything going for you, and now it just seems like it all just fell apart after you met Nigel," Chassy said.

"Yeah, it fell apart, Chassy, more than you know. But this started before I met Nigel. You two don't know everything, okay? I just don't wanna talk about it all right now. The bottom line is that Greg and I are getting a divorce and I just think it's the right thing to do. I feel this has been a long time coming."

"It's cold and lonely out here being a single woman, Lisa, I'm telling you that right now," Sharita warned.

"Yeah, and even more when you have kids trying to find someone decent. You're lucky you don't have any," Chassy said.

"Look, I'm not looking for anyone to be with after this divorce from Greg is final. I need to take time for myself. I just feel so free already from all of the bullshit that's constantly plagued our marriage. If I thought we were meant to be together forever then I would've never filed for divorce. Nothing lasts forever anyway."

Sharita and Chassy once again looked at each other.

"Only you know if you truly made the right decision, Lisa," Sharita said, as Chassy nodded in agreement.

Later on that evening while eating a fast-food meal and sitting at the kitchen table, Lisa wrote in her diary:

I did it. I filed for divorce. I didn't think I was going to at first and even hesitated about it, but I felt like it had to be done. Greg and I are officially getting a divorce, and I'm not gonna lie, I thought I'd never say this at the beginning of our marriage. He was served the papers this morning at his place of work and came into our former home and cussed me out about it during his lunch break. He was understandably upset and I expected for him to be, but he knows deep down inside that this is for the best.

I believe we were done a long time ago, and everyone is wondering how our little perfect marriage got so bad and is now ending in a divorce. Well, as they now know, it was far from perfect, and I wasn't gonna be stressed out anymore from this day forward trying to make something work that was just not gonna work anymore. We didn't even go to counseling like what we said we were gonna do and when I mentioned it to him, he said he didn't have time and that we didn't need it. Like I told Sharita and Chassy, I just wasn't happy anymore, and yeah, I admit to me talking constantly to Nigel made me really see that.

I already feel free from everything. I'm just glad to be starting a new life unattached from everything. My parents are pissed

at me for divorcing him and so is everyone, but they're not
me and don't know how I really felt all of those years with
Greg, but now they know because of what I did today.

She was jumped out of her thoughts by her phone ringing. She
looked at it to see who it was.

Nigel.

"Nigel, hi. How are you?"

"Hey, baby. The question is, how are you?"

"I'm fine, just fine."

"Are you really? Because I heard it through the grapevine that
you had some papers served to your man this morning. Is it true?"

She took a deep breath. "Yes, it's true."

"Damn, girl. I thought you were happy with him?"

"Well, as you see I really wasn't. And it took me to meet you and
realize just how unhappy I really was. Then I finally caught him
cheating on me. I just don't wanna have to take any shit from him
anymore. I admitted to him that I cheated on him with you, but now
we can both do anything we want."

"And it feels good already, doesn't it?"

"Yeah, I have to admit it does."

"Where are you right now?"

"I'm at a house my parents own that hasn't been rented out yet.
Greg kicked me out of the house after he confronted me today during
his lunch break about divorcing him. I'm here by myself," she hinted.

"Want some company?"

"Sure, I would love it."

"Um, it's not in a bad neighborhood, is it?"

"No, not at all."

"Okay, give me the address and I'll be right there."

CHAPTER THIRTY-THREE

"I'm sorry I don't have anything here for you to drink except bottles of water. I haven't had time to go grocery shopping yet," Lisa said, as she sat down at the kitchen table with Nigel.

"It's cool, baby. I'm good," he replied. He kept staring at her.

"What?" she asked, and then nervously took a sip of her water.

"I just can't believe you did what you did today, that's all. I thought you really loved the man."

She sighed. "I think a part of me will always love him, but it just wasn't a good idea for us to be married anymore."

"But you thought so not too long ago, otherwise you wouldn't have come to me for $100,000 to save your marriage."

"I know, don't remind me," she said, and then took another sip of her water. "That was when I thought it was something worth saving. Greg obviously didn't give that much of a damn about our marriage if he cheated on me with another woman in the bed we slept in, and I cheated on him with you, so it showed me *and* him both that things just fell apart between us and I just feel at this point there is no fixing it. We're always gonna fight about cheating on each other and every-thing and I just didn't wanna have to deal with it anymore."

"I definitely understand that. But does he think you left him for me?"

She sighed. "Yeah, I know he does, and the reason why I know that is because he said he knows where I took a wrong turn at in our marriage and how if I thought the grass was greener on the other side then I can go over there and that he was not gonna hold me back. I know he was talking about you, Nigel, even though he never said your name."

He nodded with a slight grin. "But did you make it clear to him that I did not tell you to divorce him for me? That we're not seeing each other? I hope you made that clear to him, Lisa."

"No, I didn't make it clear to him, Nigel, but my cousin and best friend asked me if my divorcing Greg had something to do with you and I told them it didn't; not sure if they believed me or not. But this had everything to do with me not being happy in my marriage to him anymore and I don't care what he says, he wasn't all that happy either because if he was then we wouldn't have cheated on each other."

"That's true. I just don't wanna be the cause of a woman ending her marriage because you know I had nothing to do with it."

"I know you didn't, Nigel. Like I said, your name wasn't brought up once when Greg and I talked this afternoon. He can only assume I left him for you, he has absolutely no proof."

"Did you?" he asked again, as he stared at her in suspense.

"Hey, I don't mean to interrupt y'alls conversation, I just wanted to know if I could have something to drink?" a man asked who seemed to have come out of nowhere.

Lisa looked surprised to see him. "Um, yes," she said as she got up and went to her kitchen counter and got him a bottle of water. "Here you go."

"Thank you, Lisa," he replied with a smile.

"Lisa, this is Russell Stymie," Nigel said with a smile.

"Nice to meet you, Russell," Lisa replied with a smile.

They shook hands.

"Nice to meet you, too. Courtesy of the High-Nine-Figure Man," Russell replied with a smile, and winked at her. "I'll be back in the SUV."

Lisa tried not to show any shock. "Oh, my God! Is . . . he?"

"The one who killed Pierce? You got it! POW!" he said with a laugh.

She didn't think this was funny. "How come he's here?"

"He's my right-hand man, baby," Nigel said. "I didn't know if you were telling the truth about what kind of a neighborhood this was and I didn't wanna come here alone—but you're right, it's nice and quiet. But it's not all like what you were used to living in when you were with Greg, right?"

"Yeah, you're right. We lived in a 4,200 square-foot home with a beautiful French wrought-iron double staircase, a pool in the back-yard, everything. It was beautiful and perfect for the two of us. This is a huge step down, but this is only temporary."

"And why is that?"

"Because I don't plan on staying here for that long. I do plan on getting a job since I haven't worked since high school, and just trying to work things out for myself. I'm lucky that I was able to move into a house and not some bad apartment, you know?"

"No, I actually don't know. I've never had to live in an apartment, much less a bad one. I've always lived in big, beautiful homes. Not too many people regardless of color can say that."

"Yeah, you're right, they can't. But I wanted this divorce and I'm not changing my mind about it. I feel that once it's finalized that I'll have a second chance at everything, but I had to take that first step and I did."

"There's always a second chance at everything, I definitely agree with that because that's what I feel I have now, and let me tell you, there's no better feeling than this. Good luck."

. . .

Lisa sat back at the kitchen table an hour later as she wrote in her diary:

Nigel just left here. He actually called me while I was writing my previous entry. He wanted to know if it was true about me filing from divorce from Greg, and he said he believes me because he saw for himself that I'm in this house all by myself. I also formally met the man who killed Pierce, and I got very scared for a second because I thought he was gonna hurt me because he knows I witnessed it, but he's actually a very nice guy. I just wish he hadn't killed him because there was nothing worth him killing him over. I felt like they were both warning me to still keep quiet about what I'd witnessed even though I'm divorcing Greg.

But Nigel and I talked about second chances, and I feel we both have one. I know I just filed for divorce today, so hopefully as the days and weeks and months go on we can have more than just a platonic relationship even though we have had sex a few times. But I'm pretty much free to do whatever I want, and this is feeling so good to me already. It's clear Nigel really cares about me because if he didn't then there is no way he would've called me to ask me how I was much less coming over here to see for himself. And no, we did not have sex, but now I no longer have to feel bad and guilty about it the next time we do.

CHAPTER THIRTY-FOUR

"Wow, Lisa. You've probably had the fastest divorce I've ever seen. Most people's divorces drag on for months and even over a year," Chassy said, as she and Lisa got ready for a party Nigel invited the two of them to at one of his restaurants that also doubled as a nightclub.

"Yeah, it went very fast—just a month—because it was completely uncontested on both of our parts. We just agreed to everything and since we never had kids we didn't have to worry about child support or child custody or anything, so everything went the way it should've. I have to admit Greg still looked very mad at me in court, but he knows damn well this was for the best, and now I can officially celebrate."

Chassy smiled. "I have to admit, Lisa, you do seem happier now than you did before, but it seemed as if you got happy again once you met Nigel."

"Nigel has made me very happy, and I know now since we're both divorced we can really have fun with each other and not have to hide anymore from our now ex-spouses. Chassy, I can't tell you how good I feel. I feel like I've been with Greg my whole life. I felt like I never had the chance to be free to be able to do what I've wanted when I wanted. I feel like now I have that independence and he has it as well."

"Well, Lisa, I'm glad you feel the way you do, but I'm telling you this single life isn't all what it's cracked up to be. You see how me and my second baby daddy didn't get along after all and broke up for the hundredth time it seems. I heard he has a new girlfriend."

"I'm sorry, Chassy," Lisa said, and then applied her lipstick.

"Don't be, I'm used to it. I just don't wanna see all of this shit happening to you now that's been happening to me and so many other women out here. Trust me, you never get used to it. I think all of us want that stability of marriage and a happier life for ourselves and our children."

"Well, as you see that marriage isn't all what it's cracked up to be so there was nothing for anyone to hope so much for, especially when your spouse cheated on you all the time and I admit I did the same, but now we're free to do what we want. And I don't plan on bad shit to happen because now I'm gonna do whatever I can to be Nigel's girl."

Chassy gave her a shocked look. "Lisa? So soon? Why do you wanna be his girl so soon? The ink on your divorce papers aren't even dry and you're talking about becoming his girl?"

"Why wait?"

"Because it's gonna look like you were secretly seeing him the whole time," she replied.

"Well, we know we were seeing each other as friends, even though he doesn't consider any females his friends. I don't see this as rushing into anything since we already know each other and know each other pretty well. This is why he invited me to his party tonight. He said it's a celebration of both of us being divorced."

"Wait, he invited only you?"

"He told me to bring a friend so that's why I'm bringing you, Chassy. I would've brought Sharita as well but she had to work at the last minute. I knew you would wanna go," she said, and slipped on her Valentino Rockstud black shoes with glistening gold studs.

"Yeah, sure. I'm all down for any chance to party with people who I would never get a chance to party with otherwise. I just sometimes wonder if I would really fit in."

"You'll always fit in with me, and when it gets serious between Nigel and me, imagine the kind of lifestyle I'll be living!" she said with excitement.

"I didn't see anything wrong with the lifestyle you lived when you were married to Greg, but I digress," Chassy said. "Are you ready to go? Because I have a feeling it's gonna be very crowded there and we wanna be able to get in."

"Nigel's parties usually are. But remember he personally invited me and said this party is for the two of us to celebrate our divorces, so of course we're not gonna have any problems getting in, Chassy. I can't wait to *finally* be all over him tonight in public!"

"Claim him, girl! Claim him!" Chassy said, as they laughed and walked out the door.

"Wow! It's more crowded here than I thought! And look at all of these beautiful, exotic cars lining the sides of the road, Chassy. This is the life I'm gonna soon be living with Nigel! I'm so excited!" Lisa said, as she pulled up to the front to valet her SUV.

Chassy grinned at her. "It's the life, no doubt. I guess I'll just be living vicariously through you because there's no way I'll be living like this."

"Never say never, Chassy," she said, as she checked herself out in her mirror once again. "How do I look?"

"Beautiful," Chassy replied. *Like all of the other women I see out here,* she thought.

They got out of the car and skipped the line as they walked up to the front door.

A well-dressed man wearing a black Tom Ford suit stopped them.

"Names?" he asked with a curt tone.

"Lisa Everett and Chassy King," Lisa said with a smile.

He looked at his iPad. "I don't see your names on here," he informed her.

Lisa's mouth dropped as Chassy looked at her. "Could you please check again? I personally know Nigel. He invited me and my friend to this party. He even said it was for us to celebrate our—"

"Lisa," Chassy interrupted her. "Chill, okay?"

The man glared at her with an eyeroll and adjusted his speaker headset. "Front door. Get Nigel for me."

Lisa and Chassy looked at each other.

"He's not taking any messages from the front door?" he asked in confusion.

"Let's go," Chassy mumbled to Lisa.

"No, we're getting in. Let him work it out," Lisa said, as she tried not to show her anger and embarrassment that Nigel forgot to put her on the guest list.

"Bitch ain't getting' in!" a scantily-dressed female bystander said who stood in a group with four other women.

They all laughed as they nodded in agreement.

Fuck you, Lisa thought.

"Sorry, ladies. You'll have to wait in line. Nigel is not taking any calls from the front door tonight since this is a private party. If your name is not on the list you can't get in," he informed her.

"Then what is the line for?" Chassy asked.

"That's for people who want to get it once all of the people on the guest list are in," he informed her. "But it's no guarantee that any of you will."

"This is a mistake! He obviously forgot to have his people add me and my friend here!" Lisa said.

"Sorry, if you want a chance at getting in you'll have to stand in line, but like I said, there is no guarantee that you will," he told her.

Lisa looked at the mile-long line.

"C'mon, let's go," Chassy said. "This is bullshit."

They walked away from the front door while people laughed at them.

Lisa got on her phone to call Nigel. She couldn't believe this was happening.

No answer.

Chassy looked at her. "He's not answering?"

"No," she replied as she shook her head. "This was obviously a mistake. And he told me he would keep his phone on in case I wanted to call him, and now he acts as if he doesn't wanna answer?" She called him again.

Straight to voice mail.

"I don't believe this shit!" she said.

"Let's get out of here, Lisa. This shit isn't worth it. We can have a nice night out without having to be here. This isn't the only thing that's going on tonight."

"This is the only place I wanna be tonight! This is bullshit that we weren't on the list! He's gonna hear it from me about this!" she hissed.

"I wouldn't get so mad about this, Lisa. Maybe it was a mistake; I believe it was. Shit happens. Just talk to him about it later on when the party is over. Take a few days to calm down. I hate to see you like this."

"This is as calm as I'm gonna be!" she angrily replied.

"Something smells good," Chassy said, trying to change the subject. "I think I know the restaurant it's coming from and it's not Nigel's. Let's cut through this alley." She grabbed Lisa's hand. "This is the cleanest alley I've ever been through."

As they walked through the alley, a door swung open from the side of one of the buildings.

"Hey, ladies," a man said who held a cigarette in his hand.

"Hey," Chassy said with a smile.

"Y'all here for Nigel Foreman's party?" he asked, and then lit up his cigarette.

"Yes!" Lisa replied.

He held the door open. "C'mon then, if you wanna get in."

Lisa and Chassy looked at each other in shock.

"Are you serious?" Lisa asked.

"Yeah, c'mon. I'm just out here for a smoke since Nigel doesn't allow smoking in any of his establishments. I'm just here with a friend who's a friend of Nigel."

They went up to the door and walked right in.

"Where's everyone?" Chassy asked.

"Just follow the music," he said with a smile as he still held the door.

"Thank you," Lisa said with a smile.

"No problem, baby," he said, and closed the door behind him.

"Are we really in?" Chassy asked as they walked towards the music as it got louder and louder.

"We're in!" Lisa said excitedly. "I don't believe this!"

"So, are you gonna give Nigel a piece of your mind?"

"No, now that we're in. I believe it was a mistake, so I'll just let him know that and that will be the end of it. No use in being mad about it."

They reached the main area of the party, and they knew this was a party fit for a man like Nigel, with beautifully shaped women in premier designer dresses and shoes while clutching on to expensive evening bags, to men in their premier designer looks as well. Waiters and waitresses walked around serving drinks and mouthwatering hors d'oeuvres. No one looked broke and struggling, and that was the way Nigel wanted it to be at his parties.

"Do you see him?" Chassy asked, as she snatched one of the delicious looking hors d'oeuvres off one of the plates and ate it. "Damn, this tastes expensive!"

"I don't see him yet, and I'm not leaving until I do. I'll say what I wanna say to him while we're in private because this is not the time to argue, plus, I don't wanna make myself look bad as well as him in public because that's never a good look. This is a party, and how would I look arguing with him at a party he says he's having where we're both here to celebrate our new lives as being single once again?"

"Yeah, right," Chassy said, and then took a drink off of the tray and took a sip.

Suddenly, a door swung open right in front of them and Nigel walked out with a beautiful woman all over him! He didn't see Lisa as they laughed and talked as he held both of their empty glasses of champagne with his left hand and had his right arm wrapped around her waist.

Lisa stopped where she was as Chassy starcd at her. "NIGEL!" she said, as tried to catch up to him as Chassy stayed by her side.

Nigel and the woman looked back at her.

"Hey," he replied, and turned back around to continue on back towards the main area of the party.

Lisa caught up to him. "Can we talk?"

"Not now. Excuse me," he said, and continued on with the woman still hanging on to him.

"Ni—" Lisa said.

"Lisa, let's go. For real this time," Chassy said, as she gave her a look that only a best friend could give.

Lisa sighed as she watched as Nigel and the woman who was all over him disappear around the corner.

CHAPTER THIRTY-FIVE

"Lisa, I know I'm your best friend, so I will never lie to you," Chassy said, as she drove them home since Lisa was too upset to drive.

"I know," she said, as she stared out the window.

"I think you need to leave him alone for good. Look at the way he treated you at a party he claims he invited you to tonight?"

She looked at her. "What do you mean *claim*, Chassy? He *did* invite us to the party tonight. There was obviously some mix-up or mistake with the guest list. He told me he had our names on the list."

"Are you sure? Did he double check?"

"What? Obviously not, Chassy. Look, I don't wanna make a big deal out of this, okay? I'm too mad right now. I just don't appreciate him acting like an asshole towards me when I took all of this time to get ready for a party that he told me he invited me to and to celebrate our divorces."

"C'mon, Lisa, don't be naïve, okay? You should've known there were gonna be a ton of other women there competing for his attention, and beautiful ones at that. From what I saw when we were inside, I didn't see any unattractive women. They were all there for Nigel except me. I'm not saying that you can't compete, Lisa, it's just that you just got a divorce so I think you should take things slow. And didn't you say Nigel told you he has no interest in getting remarried?"

"Yes," she replied as she looked back out her window.

"Well, there you go. If you're interested in getting remarried again then Nigel shouldn't even be a consideration. I think he completely disrespected you tonight, and it was clear he had no interest in formally meeting me. He knew I was with you."

"I'm sorry about that, Chassy. Because that's what I wanted to do was introduce him to you and it's like he acted like he couldn't be bothered with me. I have to admit this is not the way I thought the night would be."

"Well, you never can tell how any night will be, but it's clear that it's just not about this night with him, Lisa. He's obviously like this all the time. He's just not a good man to even want as a friend, I feel. Women who are involved with him are only fooling themselves if they think they're the only ones in his life, and everyone knows they all want him because they know that's their instant access to the ultimate life. But you know, I'll pass if the man is someone who acts like Nigel. It's not worth it to me."

"I understand you feeling that way because a lot of women do. But that's just it, I know I'm not the only one in his life. He's told me a lot that he can give any woman the world if she wants it, but she has to know how to act."

"And he's said that line to millions of women, so please don't get caught up in that shit with him. Like I said, there are plenty of other men out there who are very high value, power producers, Lisa, and they don't have to be as wealthy as Nigel, but they're good men looking for good women like you. Since it didn't work out with Greg after all, maybe it will work out with one of them in the future."

She sighed. "I don't know. All I do know is that I need to talk to Nigel about tonight because he needs to know how I feel. If I don't talk to him about this then I'm the one who's defeated, not him. He was the only reason why I came there tonight."

"Do what you gotta do," Chassy said and shook her head. *What is it that she can't see about him?* she thought.

Lisa sat in her bed as she wrote in her diary about her disappointing night:

> This night didn't go at all like the way I expected it to go, and it all started with Chassy and me being denied entry into the party due to our names not being on the guest list. I practically begged and pleaded with the front doorman that I knew Nigel and he said I was on the list, but when he tried to contact Nigel he informed us he wasn't taking calls from the front door. The doorman was an asshole, and Nigel was even a bigger asshole.
>
> And I only knew that because I thought luck would have it that Chassy wanted to cut through an alley and a man who was at Nigel's party opened the door since he had to go outside to smoke . . . and he let us in. Didn't know us at all.
>
> But now I wish I didn't go in at all because as we walked towards where the main action was at, Nigel happened to walk out of a room with a racially-ambiguous looking woman, and when I called his name he just turned around really quick and said, "Hey" and that was it while this woman hung all over him, something that I embarrassingly told Chassy *I* wanted to do with him tonight. I still tried to talk to him, but it was clear he didn't want to since he bluntly told me, "Not now" and continued to walk away from me with that woman.
>
> I can't even tell you how embarrassed I was, and when Chassy suggested that we leave I had to concede. I was mad

and embarrassed and so upset that he acted as if he was gonna spend time with me at this party and that we were gonna "celebrate" our divorces together, but it was clear his celebration started without me and he could've cared less whether I showed up or not.

Chassy said in the car on the way home that I should leave him alone for good, but I just don't think that's a hundred percent necessary. No, I'm not his girlfriend so it's like I really can't get mad when he's with other women, but I just can't get over the fact that he didn't care at all that there was a mess up with the guest list, and he acted as if he didn't have time to talk to me just for a few minutes since he invited me. I wasn't gonna talk to him the entire time I was there like how I initially said I was going to.

I think Chassy is right. I'm newly divorced and I've seen very fast how the single life isn't at all what it's cracked up to be, but I have faith that it will get better because it was better than staying in an unhappy marriage.

CHAPTER THIRTY-SIX

"Well, it's nice to know I didn't miss anything last night," Sharita said, as her and Lisa, as well as Chassy, sat over at Lisa's house as they ate lunch.

"Yeah, you really didn't," Chassy said. "I still couldn't believe we got in after all, all because of that man going out there to smoke."

"And I thought since that happened that it was gonna be a great night, but it was not to be," Lisa said, as she stared down at her drink.

"And how do you honestly feel about him now, Lisa, that he totally disrespected you like that?" Sharita asked.

"Yeah, and especially in front of that black, French, and Japanese-looking thot," Chassy said.

Lisa sighed. "I don't like what he did, okay? He definitely ruined my mood and night to wanna stay there, I'm not gonna lie, especially since we had to go through a roundabout way of getting in because of the mix-up on the guest list."

"I call that bullshit," Sharita said.

"What? Why are you saying that, Sharita? You weren't there," Lisa said.

"Well, I was there and I have to agree with her even though she wasn't there," Chassy said with a grin.

"Why?" Lisa angrily asked.

"Because you had absolutely no proof that Nigel really had our names put on that list, Lisa. He probably just told you that just so you would show up. Maybe he didn't do it with bad intentions, but it can't be proven that he had it done."

Lisa sat back and shook her head. "I just wanna forget about it. I felt so stupid there last night."

"Tell me about it," Chassy said. "I know where I fit in and don't fit in, and that party was definitely a place where I didn't fit in at, not at all."

"Hey, we may not be wealthy, but I'd rather be like this than be chasing around a man who is so out of my league that he would never even consider me a girlfriend much less a wife," Sharita said.

"Well, he's not considering any woman his wife since he told me that he's never getting remarried," Lisa informed them.

"But wouldn't you like to get remarried?" Chassy asked.

Sharita looked at her and raised her eyebrows.

"Yeah, I would like it. But I just got a divorce and that's what we were supposed to be there celebrating."

"You didn't have to go celebrating that with him, Lisa, you could've just stayed here. And if I didn't have to work last night we all could've stayed here and celebrated if you wanted, but it doesn't seem like you truly wanna celebrate your divorce. You only seemed to have agreed to do that because of Nigel suggesting it."

Lisa sighed. "Yeah, I did. Honestly, the thought of it felt very uncomfortable to me, because I know Greg wasn't out celebrating our divorce."

"I still follow him on all of his social media pages and you're right, he wasn't. He hasn't been on social media much since the two of you haven't been together," Sharita said.

"I really don't care what he does anymore so I would appreciate it if you don't tell me," Lisa said.

"No problem," Sharita said with a grin. "But back to Nigel. Like Chassy said, I think you need to leave him alone for good. He's not even worth you just hanging out with and having sex with on occasion or whatever. That should've told you everything you needed to know about him last night when he acted as if he didn't even have time to even talk to you."

"And acted as if he didn't even wanna formally meet me," Chassy said. "Wow, I guess I really don't look good enough for him even to meet and that's it."

"Damn, that was rude as hell. What an asshole!" Sharita said, and took a sip of her drink.

"And I said I'm sorry about that, Chassy."

"No problem, Lisa. It just told me what kind of a person he is, and just to think I had a big crush on him. I guess it's true what they say, never try to meet your crushes, idols, whatever, because it almost always ends in heartbreak," Chassy said.

"Exactly, Chassy," Sharita said, and then turned and looked at Lisa. "And we don't want Nigel breaking your heart, Lisa."

"Thanks for your concern," she replied. *But in a lot of ways he already did,* she thought.

CHAPTER THIRTY-SEVEN

It'd been weeks since the party, and Lisa hadn't heard from Nigel since, but she wasn't going to dwell on it anymore on what'd happened the last night she'd seen him. She decided to pursue her master's degree at the same college she'd gotten her bachelor's from, so she enrolled in some classes to get herself going and to lift her spirits.

While in the middle of studying for one of her classes, she received a call.

Nigel.

She was reluctant to pick up the phone so she let it ring until it stopped. She waited for a message. It never came. *I just don't know if I wanna talk to him anymore,* she thought.

Her phone rang again a minute later.

Nigel, again.

She knew he probably wasn't gonna stop calling her. "Hi, Nigel."

"Hey, what's up, girl. I tried to call you a minute ago. What's going on?"

"Oh, I was in the bathroom and didn't hear it," she lied.

"Yeah, okay. Well, I wanted to know if you were free to have lunch right now? I have the day off and was gonna have it at my restaurant but didn't wanna eat alone."

She perked up. "Sure, I would love to!"

"Why do you sound so excited? It's just lunch," he said with a chuckle.

"Um, because I'm hungry and I know your restaurant has great food."

"Yeah, it does, all of them do. I'll pick you up in about an hour, okay?"

"Sounds great, Nigel."

"Wow, it's not every day I get picked up in a Bugatti just to go to lunch!" Lisa said excitedly, as Nigel sped down the road on his way to the restaurant.

"Yeah, not every person in this world can say that," he replied with a smile. "I just got this car so I wanted to show it off. It's my second one from this brand. This is what hard work looks like, baby."

"And it's a beautiful look!"

They laughed.

"Yeah, I'm working hard again because I wanna get back out there and get a job even though I'm receiving good alimony from Greg. I hate sitting around the house."

"And that's what I like to hear. I don't like lazy women. I like women who have something to bring to the table and ones who don't act as if they're entitled to everything. I admit that I need to stop saying I can give any woman the world because it does make them feel entitled."

"It does, Nigel. Any woman can get used to your lifestyle. I feel privileged just sitting in this car going to lunch with you."

"Glad you appreciate it."

"I definitely do."

Several minutes later, they arrived at the restaurant . . . and it was the same one he had the party at. She tried not to show her disappointment since she wanted to forget about this place since it was one of her worst nights since being officially single.

Nigel pulled up to the valet. He looked at her. "Something wrong?"

"Nothing's wrong," she replied with a fake smile. "I just thought we were gonna eat at one of your other restaurants."

"Which one?" he asked with a slight grin.

"I don't know . . . Denise's?"

"You've had that before so that's why I decided to come here."

"That's true. It's fine, really. I look forward to it."

After a round of Nigel shaking hands with the other customers in the restaurant, they were finally seated in a private section in the restaurant which was usually reserved for VIP or for Nigel himself as well as his family and friends. Russell stood at a distance to make sure no one bothered them while they were here.

"Order anything you want. The meal is free since I own the place," he replied with a smile.

"That's nice to know. Thank you," she replied as she looked at the menu. *But how special is this really if he only took me here so he wouldn't have to pay for it? It's truly only lunch, obviously nothing special to him,* she thought.

The private waiter came over to them and took their orders for drinks and brought them to the table minutes later.

"So, about the last time I was here," she said, and then took a hard sip of her Cosmopolitan.

"What about it?" he asked with a smile.

"Well, for starters, I didn't get to spend the time with you that I wanted to."

"And?" he asked, then took a sip of his hard liquor.

She slightly gasped since she couldn't believe that he'd said this. "I just feel the night could've been a lot better but it wasn't. Did you know that Chassy and I couldn't get in?"

"Wait, I'm confused. Then how did the two of you get in?"

"Through the back door in the alley. And it was only because a man at your party decided to go out there and smoke."

He sighed. "I need to keep that back door guarded."

"But that's not the point, Nigel. Your front doorman was an asshole, excuse me, but he was. He didn't do anything about something I felt he should've done something about."

"And what was that?" he asked.

She couldn't believe he'd said this. This showed her that he really did not care about what went on that night. "He should've personally gone to you and checked with you about my name not being on the guest list, but all he said was when he tried to contact you that you weren't taking any calls from the front door."

"I wasn't," he confirmed, and took another sip of his drink.

She tried to control her growing anger. "You didn't care that my name was not on the guest list? You told me that it was on there and all I had to do was come up to the front and tell the front doorman my name and my friend's name."

"Look, Lisa, I don't know why you're making a big deal out of this. Shit happens. Someone obviously fucked up on something and it's not my fault. That night has been over with for pretty much a month now. I just wanted to take you out to lunch since I haven't seen you since then."

"And I did forget about it until you called me. I only went there that night because of you. We were supposed to celebrate our divorces together."

"I never said that."

"Yes you did!" she snapped.

"Do you wanna eat here? Because you can go someplace else to eat and I'll have another woman sitting here in minutes, so I suggest you tone it down."

She tried hard to suppress the tears that were welling up in her eyes. "I just wanted you to know how I felt about that night. I think you had a right to know."

"And you told me so that's the end of it."

But she didn't feel it was the end of it, she felt it was just the beginning. She was at the beginning of her single life and wanted to be respected as a newly single woman albeit a single divorcee.

"I just got one more thing I wanna ask you?"

"What's that?" he asked, and took another sip of his drink.

"Who was that woman you were with while I tried to get your attention?"

"What woman?" he asked with confusion.

She wasn't gonna go around in circles with him about this. "Nigel, you know what woman I'm talking about. The one that you were with when you acted as if you didn't wanna talk to me. You know, you really embarrassed me in front of my best friend. I didn't even get the chance to introduce you to her. After all, you told me to bring a friend, so it would've been appropriate for me to introduce you to her."

"Well, first of all, the woman that I was with was none of your business, Lisa, if you want me to be frank with you about it. She's not my girlfriend and neither are you. But she knows how to stay in her place and I suggest you learn that, too, as a newly single woman. I can do what I wanna do and I'm not making any apologies for it. We're both single so we can now be open and free from all the bull-shit that plagued us during our marriages, right?"

She sighed. "Yeah, you're right."

"And the last thing I wanna deal with is some bullshit from a woman that is not even my girlfriend—understand?"

"Yeah, I understand."

"So, since we got that out the way, I was wondering what I could do to make it up to you about not spending time with you at the party that night."

She suddenly perked up once again. "Well, my mom's monthly soul food feast is coming up the Sunday after the next. I would love for you to come as my date."

"I don't do those family things, especially for a woman I'm not married to," he informed her.

She was crushed. "I understand."

"But I'll make an exception in this case," he informed her.

She shrieked! "Oh, my God, Nigel! Are you serious? For real?"

"Yeah, for real. I love soul food—what black person doesn't? Just tell me where it is and I'll be there."

"Or maybe we can go together? I know my parents would love to meet you."

"Why? We're not dating, Lisa."

She sighed once again. "I know we're not, Nigel. They know that I know you and there's nothing like me coming there with you when all of the other times I went with Greg since we were married."

"Is he gonna be there?" he asked with a grin.

She smirked. "Absolutely not. He's officially my ex-husband. He has no reason to come to events that's held by my side of the family just like I stopped going to the ones held by his side of the family once we officially divorced."

"Makes sense. So just give me the info I need and I'll make it up to you by letting you show me off to your family," he said with a smile.

"And I can't wait to do it!" she said excitedly.

Hour later after her lunch date with Nigel, she wrote in her diary:

I can't believe I had lunch with Nigel. He called me. And just when I was trying to move on with my life since my divorce. But I took the opportunity to tell him how I felt about that night of the party that he acted as if he didn't wanna spend any time with me at because of all places we could've went to lunch at this afternoon, it was *there*. I felt like I was going back to the scene of the crime or something, and I felt like it was a crime because of the way he treated me there . . . but he said he would make it up to me by coming to my mom's soul feast the Sunday after the next. I can't wait to see everyone's faces when he shows up there because I did tell Chassy and Sharita after he'd dropped me off here that he was coming to it and they said they can't wait as well, and my mom especially said she can't wait since she knew about him when I was married to Greg.

I enjoyed lunch after I got it out of the way about how I felt that night, and he was defiant about it at first, but it was clear he was defeated because he knew how he acted. But the one thing he never said to me that still gets to me about that night . . . he never said he was sorry.

CHAPTER THIRTY-EIGHT

THE MONTHLY SUNDAY SOUL FEAST WAS UNDERWAY, AND IT WAS ONE OF THE largest turnouts ever . . . and for one reason. Everyone wanted to see and meet the High-Nine-Figure Man in person and to get their own selfies with a man they never thought would be attending an event that they attended as well.

Lisa wanted to look her best, and was wearing a new outfit and shoes for the occasion, courtesy of Nigel. She stood in a circle with Chassy and Sharita as they talked and laughed as the savory scent of the self-proclaimed best soul food lingered in the air while the sounds of a game blasted from an outside TV while trying to compete with music blaring from the speakers.

"Girl, that Chanel outfit is *everything*!" Sharita said to Lisa. "I would still wanna talk to Nigel too if he spent that kind of money on me just so I could buy outfits like that all the time!"

"Thanks, Sharita. He said I could have whatever I wanted for this event and this look caught my eye. I couldn't believe I was in Chanel with him and was able to get whatever I wanted all because of him. Never have I been able to do that."

"Most of us in this world haven't, Lisa," Chassy said. "And I've never seen a pair of leather shorts that cost $5,250!"

"Hardly anyone has," Lisa replied with a grin. "You know I would've never been able to afford a pair of shorts like these if it wasn't for him. I'm seeing the perks of being in a relationship with him."

Sharita and Chassy looked at each other.

"So, you're *officially* in a relationship with him? Don't you think this is kind of fast?" Sharita asked.

"Well, it's not official, it's just that we have been spending time together and he told me when he took me shopping that he doesn't take just any woman shopping. He said he fools around with a lot of women as we all know, but taking her shopping is something he only does when he really likes her," Lisa replied.

"Likes her? To buy you a whole freakin' Chanel outfit and a bag and shoes and jewelry is more than liking someone, Lisa!" Sharita said.

Chassy laughed. "Yeah, I agree! I'm freakin' jealous, I can't lie. I didn't know what to think of him since you've met him, Lisa, since he always gives me mixed feelings about him, but it finally seems like he's showing a true interest in you."

"Well, we've had a secret interest in each other since the day we met, we just couldn't really show it and be out in the open with it until now," Lisa replied. "I think I'm drinking too much. Gotta go to the bathroom."

Minutes later, she walked into the bathroom. She got out her phone.

Where are you? she texted to Nigel.

A minute later, she received a response.

I'm on my way.

Okay, because we're all waiting for you. My mom doesn't want anyone to eat until you get here since you're the guest of honor, and the food is almost done.

Sounds good. Can't wait to get there. I'm hungry!

She walked out of the bathroom and ran into her mom.

"Baby, where's the main man of the event?"

"He just texted me and told me he's on his way," Lisa replied, trying to twist the messages.

"Okay, baby. Because everyone's getting hungry and know they can't eat until he gets here. If he decides to bring more than just his friends Jerry and Russell, there's plenty of food to go around."

"That's good to know, Mom, but I think it's only Russell that's coming with him since he's pretty much his best friend like Jerry and his right-hand man."

"Can't wait to meet them all," she said with a big smile.

"What kind of a man says he's gonna show and never does, Lisa? How the hell could you have divorced Greg for someone like this?" her mom said.

"I agree with your mom," her dad said. "I liked Greg from the start. The two of you had something good in the ten years you were married."

"I wasn't happy with Greg like I thought I would be and you both know how much he cheated on me, and me catching him in the act was the straw that broke the camel's back—but I didn't divorce him for Nigel."

"But you thought being with Nigel now would make you happy, right? Why, Lisa? Because he has a lot of money?" her mom asked.

Lisa continued to stare at her plate of food that she'd barely touched. The monthly event was over, and everyone had gone home.

"Just because someone has more money than someone else and can buy you fancy Chanel outfits doesn't mean they'll make you completely happy," her mom informed her. "You know what I told you several months ago about Nigel. I told you that you had a great husband—now I'm saying you *used to* have a great husband—and that you needed to stop talking and seeing Nigel, but you didn't listen. You know we raised you better than this."

"Your mom is right, Lisa. What kind of a man stands up a woman when she invited him to meet her parents as well as other friends and family? This man is no good. You're getting played by him. Greg may not have been perfect and neither are you, but this was not worth you divorcing him over," her dad said.

Lisa abruptly got up out of her seat, grabbed her purse and stormed out of the house as tears welled up in her eyes.

As tears streamed down her eyes, Lisa wrote in her diary about what'd happened today:

He stood me up. There, I said it. I feel like it was all a setup like the way he set up Pierce to be killed. I now think he had no intentions on coming to the get-together this afternoon and only bought me this outfit so I wouldn't be mad at him. I tried calling and texting him numerous times and he only responded the first time. He doesn't realize just how bad he embarrassed and humiliated me in front of my family and friends today, and to have my parents say that he was not worth me divorcing Greg over really made me mad because my divorce from Greg was not based on wanting to be with Nigel. Greg was not gonna stop doing what he was doing and I wasn't gonna put up with it anymore.

But Nigel really crossed the line with me this time. I honestly don't know if I'm gonna be able to see him again. After all, I'm single and have other options even though I'm a divorcee. I may not get someone of his wealth and status, but I feel I will end up with a much better person overall because he has shown me more than once that he doesn't respect me like the way I thought he did.

CHAPTER THIRTY-NINE

Lisa stared out at the pouring down rain while she sat in Starbucks as she browsed online. She hadn't heard from Nigel since and it'd been well over a week since the get-together, so she knew now that he had no interest in talking to her anymore because it was easy for a man like him to do whatever he wanted to do without a care or thought for someone's feelings.

She looked across the street and did a double-take . . . .

It was Nigel!

She jumped up out of her seat and ran out the door before he got into his car.

"NIGEL!!!" she said as she ran across the street as it continued to rain and rain hard.

He looked at her as Russell held an umbrella over his head. "Lisa. What's up?"

"What's up? What's up with you?! How come you stood me up at my family's monthly get-together?"

"Something came up," he said as he stared down at her.

"It didn't seem like something came up when I texted you to ask you where you were and you said you were on your way and you *never* showed! You embarrassed me, Nigel! In front of all of my friends and family! How could you do that to me?!"

"I can't talk about this right now, I need to get back to work. Excuse me," he said, as Russell opened the door for him to get inside the car.

They drove off seconds later as she stood in the same spot soaking wet.

"MOTHERFUCKER!!!" she yelled as she cried.

"And just when I started to have respect for that man, he stood you up at your parent's monthly get-together, and then acted as if he didn't wanna talk to you about it since you tried to talk to him today about it," Chassy said, as she sat a hot cup of tea in front of Lisa.

Lisa took a sip of the tea. "I know, Chassy. I just couldn't believe it when I saw him ready to get into his car across the street. I would've never seen him if I wasn't sitting by the window. He told me that 'something came up.'"

"He's full of shit," she said, and took a sip of her tea. "I'm telling you, Lisa, you need to officially leave him alone. He's gone past the point of being disrespectful to you. You can't keep giving a man like him chances and excuses for why he does what he does. He's always gonna do what he wants to do and doesn't care what anyone says. You're free from Greg now and that's what you wanted so I suggest you just take this time for yourself and fuck Nigel. There are plenty of other men out there that you can have a real relationship with who will respect you like the way you deserve to be respected."

"I know there are, Chassy, it's just that I feel I have a history with Nigel. It was easy getting a divorce since I knew I had someone who was already interested in me and I was interested in him. I know it was wrong, but when I caught Greg in the actual act of cheating on me, I knew I had every reason to go ahead and file for divorce and that I could now be free of him to be able to see Nigel whenever I wanted."

"And how has that been working out?"

She shook her head. "You know how it's been working out for me, so I don't need for you to be sarcastic right now because I really need a best friend like what you are to me."

Chassy sighed. "I know, Lisa, and I'm sorry. It's just that I've been to the two events that you've been to which has involved Nigel and he treated you very badly at his party, and he didn't even show up at your family get-together and gave some lame excuse about something coming up when you know damn well nothing came up. I know I don't fit in his world or whatever, but sometimes we just have to get in where we fit in and stop trying to be with people who clearly don't wanna seriously be with us."

She frowned. "So, what are you trying to say? That I don't fit in his world?"

"No, Lisa, I'm not trying to say that at all because if he didn't think you did he wouldn't be involved with you for this long. I just don't think that a man like Nigel has the capability of really seriously liking any woman the way she should be liked and even loved."

"Yeah, he admitted to me that he never loved Aisha and said marriage was never for him, so I get what you're saying. But—"

"There shouldn't be any more buts about him, Lisa. The man is an asshole, and I'm gonna be blunt about it because of the shit I've personally witnessed between the two of you. I can imagine how hard it is to stop seeing a man who can give a woman anything; that came up to you for the very first time when you weren't expecting it. But damn, there were obvious signs that he should've been left alone when you didn't even know him for that long, right?"

She sighed. "Yeah, you're right, Chassy. I was just so bored and lonely with my housewife life with Greg that I felt that someone like Nigel coming up to me was a one-and-a-million chance happening. He made me happy every time I saw him, and we had something in common—we were unhappy in our marriages to other people. One thing just led to another with us, and now that we're both single we can do what we want."

"And that's exactly what he's doing, Lisa, whatever *he* wants. I just don't think he wants to include you exclusively in it."

"Well, I don't expect to be exclusively with him, Chassy. I think I know better than that by now. Look, I don't know if anything will ever become serious with Nigel and me, and I know this is because he said he's not interested in getting remarried and neither am I. This is a time for us to have fun together and be open in our relationship because we're both single."

"Fun? Really? Because it just seems like you've had nothing but misery since you met him and especially now since your divorce from Greg. Look beyond him, Lisa. There are millions and millions of other men that will give you the happiness you felt you lost with Greg. Nigel is not the one."

CHAPTER FORTY

Weeks had past, and not a word from Nigel through any formal means of communication. Lisa felt that this was officially it with him since she really thought about what Chassy had said about him the day she confronted him in the pouring rain about standing her up at her parents get-together. She even met a man while she studied at Starbucks who was a high-value man, the kind she liked; the kind she was used to. They'd talked on the phone and through social media several times, but she hadn't been out with him on a date yet since she said it was still a little too soon to be actively dating.

Her phone rang.

Nigel.

She couldn't believe it. It felt like it'd been a year since she'd talked to him.

"Hello?" she said, as if she didn't know it was him.

"Hey, girl. What's up? How have you been?" he said, as if the last time he'd spoken to her was earlier that week.

"Nothing much. Just studying for my master's degree."

"Sounds great, baby. You have any free time coming up?"

"Well, yeah. I can study from anywhere and don't have any exams anytime soon."

"Then you're gonna like what I'm gonna ask you."

"What?!" she asked in an overexcited tone she couldn't even hide.

"I also have some rare free time I give myself and wanted to know if you would like to come with me on a nice exotic vacation."

She shrieked with excitement! "YES!"

He laughed. "That was fast!"

"Nigel, I can't tell you how long it's been since I've been anywhere. I know I won't be bored on this vacation with you, and since my divorce, I'm long overdue for one. Where are we going?"

"Wherever you want."

"Are you serious, Nigel? You mean *I* can decide where we can go? Oh, my God! I feel like I'm dreaming!"

"My private jet can fly us anywhere in this world, baby, so you can pick the place."

"I've been all around the world, but I haven't been everywhere. But what I like most is exotic islands. Been to Maldives and some others, so I think I would love to go to one."

"Sounds good. How about the Laucala Islands in Fiji? They're private islands."

"*Private* islands? Wow! Yes! That's perfect! Never been there!"

"Okay, sounds good, Lisa. I'll have my assistant book it for us. I'll put money in your bank account so you can buy some new clothes and shoes and whatever else you want for this trip since it'll be our first one together. It'll also be a chance for us to get to know each other and forget about everything that's happened in the past."

"I agree with that a hundred percent. I can't wait, Nigel."

CHAPTER FORTY-ONE

Against the very much founded and critical judgement and concern of her family and friends, Lisa boarded Nigel's private jet for her dream vacay, and she let the world of social media know. She also tried to let her family and friends know that everything was going to be okay and that her and Nigel had been getting along great leading up to their first vacation together. She felt that this was a sign that things could possibly get serious between the two of them, especially since he'd informed her that he only took less than one percent of the women he meets and has some kind of intimate relationship with on an exotic vacation to a private island.

She started to feel special and wanted by him all over again.

"Gotta get some pics and video for social media on the inside of this beautiful jet!" she replied with a big smile. "These haters on here think I'm faking this vacay."

Nigel laughed. "Yeah, they would think that because none of them will ever go anywhere nice and in a private jet that they own at that—not rent, *own*, big difference. I own everything I have."

"You don't have to tell me, baby!" she happily said. "Let's get some selfies together."

"No," he abruptly said as he gave her a serious look. "Leave me out of your pictures."

She tried not to show how disappointed she was that he'd said this. "But everyone knows you're taking me on this vacation. I'm only going because of you."

"That doesn't mean I want to be seen," he informed her. "I'm not a showoff, Lisa. This is the way I live. I don't need to be on social media telling and showing everyone my business. Only people who's never had anything or ones that are faking their lifestyle does that. And I hate fake-rich people."

But since she followed him she'd seen a hell of a lot of pictures with him on this plane with numerous friends and other women before and after she'd met him, but she knew if she wanted this plane to take off to their destination with her on it then she knew she'd better not argue with him.

"Okay, I understand," she finally replied.

"And you know not to take any pictures of me," Russell said with a friendly smile.

"I know," she replied as she returned a smile, but knew exactly why he didn't want any pictures taken of him as well. She couldn't believe he was still acting as if he didn't kill Pierce months before, and it was clear he had no intentions on doing any time for it . . . and neither did Nigel.

She was alone in her selfies and tried to flash a genuine smile in each one she took. Likes and comments poured in. Suddenly, she received a DM:

I see you finally got who and what you wanted. I hope you're finally happy.

Greg.

She wasn't shocked at this message at all since she knew he hadn't stopped following her, and she didn't want to block him since he wasn't harassing her in any way. She looked at Nigel as he talked on his phone as Russell watched what was on one of the TVs. The plane hadn't taken off yet.

She sighed as she tried to figure out whether or not she wanted to respond to him, but then ultimately decided not to. She had a new beginning now, and even though she wasn't happy in the beginning with everything that'd happen since she'd met Nigel, she felt that her being on this private jet and going to a private island was proof enough that Nigel still had a true interest in her, and he was willing to work things out between them for the best with forgetting about the past since they'd met and building on a new and better future with each other.

She continued to take selfies as well as pictures of the plane, as well as videos.

Nigel came back to where she was at since they were now on their way to their destination. "I know how to get you to stop taking all of these pictures and videos for a few hours."

She grinned at him. "How?"

"How about we go in my private room to talk and have some real fun?"

She laughed. "Yeah, I'm definitely down with that!"

"What are you waiting for? C'mon," he said, and grabbed her hand and pulled her up out of the seat.

Russell looked back with a huge grin. "Have fun."

"Guaranteed," Nigel said as Lisa hung all over him with a drink in her hands as she laughed.

"So, was this the first time you ever had sex in a private jet?" Nigel asked as he held her in his arms as they laid in his bed in his private room.

"Hell yeah, it is! First time for everything and it was the best sex I've ever had. Never did I think I would be flying in a private jet much less having sex with the man who owns it!"

He laughed. "Yeah, welcome to the good life, baby. Never a dull moment. *Never*."

"And I was tired of all of the dull moments I had while being married. Do you know he DM'd me while I was taking selfies on this plane?"

"He still follows you?"

"Yeah, he obviously still does. This is the first time he's said something to me on social media since I filed for divorce, so I didn't think he was still following me because I didn't care. I just wanted that part of my life to be over with when it came to him."

"What did he say?"

"He just said that he hopes I got who and what I wanted and that he hopes I'm happy now."

"You do know he was being sarcastic, right?"

"Yeah, I know, and I don't care and I showed him I didn't care by never responding to him. He can have as many whores as he wants now to fuck in his bed because I don't give a fuck. I knew he was never gonna stop doing that shit because he was doing it to me in high school and I can say with a clear conscience that I never cheated on him during high school, and you were the only one that I cheated on him with throughout our marriage, so we just didn't need to be with each other anymore."

"Yeah, it sounds like the two of you shouldn't have been. When you've had enough you've had enough. I know I did. Like I said, I'm glad to be in a new beginning just like you and I'm glad we're still talking."

She smiled and cuddled up to him some more. "And so am I."

He slowly got up as she stared at him. "I gotta use the bathroom and then talk to Russell for a bit. I'm sure you know how to keep yourself entertained."

She nodded as she still smiled. "Yeah, I do," she replied and held up her phone. "Plus, there's a nice TV in here as well."

"Knock yourself out like the sex we just had."

"That's for sure!" she replied with a laugh.

He laughed and left the room.

She took a few selfies in his bed and posted them on social media, and then watched a little bit of TV. She got up since what she was watching was boring and snooped around his room. "Wow. This room looks better than most master bedrooms in nice-size houses," she said. She looked in one of the drawers. She saw a beautiful box. She opened it and gasped so loud she covered her mouth once she had.

In this box sat a beautiful 15-carat solitaire emerald-cut diamond ring set on beautiful platinum. She'd never seen a diamond this big and up this close as it almost blinded her with its beauty, shine, and clarity. She couldn't believe this.

This can't be happening! Wow! she thought.

She peeked out the door and saw Nigel talking and laughing it up with Russell as they sat across from each other with drinks in their hands as they watched porn on the main TV. She grinned as she shook her head and closed the door, and got on her phone to call Chassy.

"Hey, girl! I know you're not on the island yet," Chassy said.

"No, I'm not," Lisa replied. "But I'm talking quietly because I have to be quiet because you're not gonna believe what I just found in the drawer in Nigel's bedroom!"

"Well, from the sounds of your voice it must be something pretty damn good because even though you're talking in a quiet tone, I can hear the excitement all in your voice."

"That's because I am, Chassy! I am! I knew there was a reason why he's taking me to this island!"

"And what's the reason, Lisa?"

"I know this seems superfast, but I found the most beautiful diamond ring! Holy shit! It's gotta be at least 15 carats, maybe more!"

"Stop lying, Lisa. I know you're excited about going to this private island with him and flying on his private jet with him, but you don't have to make up stories. I'm sure there's gonna be plenty of them you can tell me once you come back home."

"I'm not lying, Chassy! I'm gonna send you the picture of it right now!" she said, and texted her a picture of it. She waited a few seconds. "Did you get it?"

"HOLY SHIT!" Chassy responded. "Sorry for thinking you were making it up! That ring is *everything*! You think he's gonna propose to you, Lisa? Are you serious? And I'm not trying to be funny when I'm asking you this because I thought you said he didn't wanna get remarried?"

"Well, that's what he said, but this ring is clearly showing that he changed his mind! Oh, my God! I just can't believe this! We've only been knowing each other for a few months and we're both recently divorced! He had me convinced that he didn't wanna get remarried! I guess this is all a part of the surprise! Why else would he be taking me here?"

"You got a point there, but people go on vacations like that all the time just for the hell of going and getting away from things for a while. But yeah, that ring brings it to a whole other level. You know not to post that on social media, right?"

"Yes, Chassy, I know. And I suggest you delete the pic as well since I really took a big risk by sending it to you."

"Lisa, you know I'm your girl. You know I'm not gonna post it to social media or send it to anyone. Does Sharita know?"

"No, she doesn't know yet. I tried to contact her but she wasn't answering her phone and I expected that since I know she's at work."

"Well, I gotta say you're officially living the life, Lisa. I hope you thought it was all worth it."

"You say it like it's a bad thing. Nigel came up to me that day, I didn't come up to him. Yeah, things didn't go smoothly between us since we were both married at the time but there's a reason why we're still talking to each other despite everything. And it's clear that he meant it when he said about forgetting about everything that's happened in the past between us and this was our chance to start a better future together. Now I know why he said these things to me because he's gonna propose to me!"

CHAPTER FORTY-TWO

"Lisa, I honestly don't know what to say," Sharita said, as they sat at her kitchen table along with Chassy.

"Me neither, Lisa. I felt your excitement when you showed me that picture and was even more excited about seeing it in person," Chassy said.

Lisa shook her head as she wiped tears from her eyes. "It's clear he changed his mind for whatever reason. When the vacation came to an end, I thought maybe he was gonna propose to me on the way back here since he didn't do it while we were there, but then what would've been the point of that, you know? It wouldn't have made any sense. I never saw the ring again since accidentally discovering it when we were on our way there."

"Have you talked to him about this? I think since you saw the ring and it was on an accident, maybe you should just for peace of mind," Sharita suggested.

Lisa shrugged. "I don't know. I guess there was a lot of wishful thinking on my part. I admit that it's definitely too soon to accept a proposal from a man after just getting officially divorced from another. I mean, what was I thinking?"

"It's easy to think thoughts like that, Lisa. You had every reason to think that way since after all, he initiated everything by asking you if you wanted to go on an exotic vacation and letting you pick the place, then on the way there you discover a huge diamond ring in one of the drawers in his room. Hell, I would've thought I was gonna be proposed to as well!" Chassy said. "And that ring was gorgeous from the pictures you showed me."

"I would've thought the same thing, Lisa," Sharita said. "I mean, what girl wouldn't have?"

Lisa sighed as she continued to wipe tears from her eyes. "It's such a letdown, I have to admit. I know he didn't buy that ring for himself. That was clearly an engagement ring that I thought was clearly for me. I got a great taste of what my life would be like with him and felt that he wanted to finally make me officially a part of it."

"Maybe he still does, Lisa. The only way you'll know if that ring really is for you is if you ask him. I usually wouldn't suggest this, but you've already seen the ring and it seems like everything fit for a proposal that never happened. I think you'll feel better if you talk to him since you said the two of you had a nice trip despite you never being proposed to," Sharita said.

Lisa sighed once again as she stared down at her cup of hot tea. "I'll think about it."

CHAPTER FORTY-THREE

Weeks had passed, and Lisa was still seeing and speaking to Nigel, but she just didn't have enough courage to bring up something that she felt could've possibly caused him to be very upset with her about since she had no business snooping around in his drawers in his private room on the plane. She felt she was even making herself physically sick from the pressure she was putting on herself about whether or not she should've asked him about the ring, but she felt by now if he really wanted to propose to her then he would've already done so.

She came out of the bathroom after vomiting, and knew that in order to make herself feel better that she needed to forget about this once and for all. She was also under a lot of stress from school trying to get her master's degree since she hadn't been to school in well over ten years. She had a lot to do, and being proposed to so soon after a recent divorce was the last thing she should've had on her mind.

She got on her phone. "Hey, Chassy. I'm not feeling well."

"What's wrong, Lisa?"

"I think it's just all of the stress with school and Nigel and everything even though we've been getting along just fine and I wanna keep it that way."

"You still haven't told him about finding that ring he never gave to you, huh?"

She sighed. "No, I haven't, and I think it's really stressing me out, but I just don't think he needs to know after all so I'm trying not to think about it."

"Yeah, you'll take a lot of stress off of you if you just forget that you ever found it, Lisa, really."

"I know, and that's what I'm trying to do. But I was wondering if you could make me some of that homemade chicken noodle soup you learned how to make from your mom?"

"No problem at all, Lisa. I'll get on it right away and bring it to you as soon as it's done."

Over an hour later, Lisa sat in her bed as she ate some of the soup. "Love this soup, Chassy. Thanks so much again. I need to get the recipe for myself so I don't have to bug you to make any for me when I really want and need it, but I would probably never get mine to taste this good."

Chassy laughed. "That's what I said about my mom's. Even though I made this for you, I can never get mine to taste as good as hers!"

They laughed as they nodded in agreement.

"Oh, there's something else I brought over for you."

"What is it?" she asked, and scooped up some more of her soup.

Chassy dug in her purse. "This."

Lisa gave her a very confused look. "Why would I need that?"

"Lisa, come on now. Don't start playing games."

Lisa put the bowl of soup on her nightstand and took the pregnancy test box from her. "Yeah, I ran through a lot of these while I was married."

"When was your last period?"

"It should be right around the corner, but it varies. That's probably why I don't feel well and have cravings for all types of foods, you know how it is."

"Yeah, and I also know that those are some of the same symptoms of being pregnant. You have to find out, Lisa. I know you haven't mentioned it or anything, but you rarely get sick so I just wanna rule this out."

Lisa got up with the box. "For your peace of mind, I'll take it."

Minutes later, they stared at the stick.

Positive.

"You're gonna have to let him know, Lisa. The sooner, the better."

CHAPTER FORTY-FOUR

"So, what's up? What did you wanna talk to me about that couldn't wait?" Nigel asked, as him and Lisa sat in his recreation room in his house.

"I'm not gonna beat around the bush with you," she replied, and pulled the pregnancy test stick out of her purse. She handed it to him.

He took it from her, looked at it, and gave it back to her. "How do I know it's mine?"

"It's yours, Nigel. I haven't had sex with any other man but you."

"But how do I know you're serious about that especially since you're now divorced?"

"I'm serious, Nigel. I wouldn't kid about something like this. If there was another possibility out there I would let you know."

He shook his head. "I have nine kids, Lisa. I don't need any more, you know that."

"But you can afford—"

"That's not the fuckin' point!" he yelled as he jumped up.

She watched him as he shook his head and walked to the bar and made himself a drink. "I'm sorry if this upset you."

"Upset's not even the word," he replied, and took a sip of his hard liquor. "I thought you were on some shit, you know? Especially since you're single again?"

"I haven't been on anything for over a decade since I was trying to get pregnant when I was married, but it never happened. I hate to say it like this but it was never meant to happen between Greg and me, but it was meant to happen between us."

"I don't wanna hear that shit, Lisa! I told you, I have nine kids — five by my ex-wife and four by three baby mamas even though one of them are dead. I don't need any more drama with this kid shit!"

"I'm not trying to cause any drama, Nigel, you know that. It's just that I couldn't go on without telling you because you have every right to know."

"And I thought you were different, Lisa."

She gave him a shocked look. "Different? What do you mean?"

"That you wouldn't be the type that would try and trap a man into wanting to be with you by getting pregnant by him."

"We both did this, Nigel, and you know it!"

"Don't start arguing with me about this shit or you're gonna have to get the fuck out of my house, I mean it!"

"Sorry," she said with her head lowered.

He shook his head as he sat back down on another sofa. "Well, even though I don't want you to have this child like I told the other three baby mamas, I can't stop you from having it and if it's proven to mine, I'll support it because I don't run from my responsibilities."

She smiled as tears welled up in her eyes. "Thank you."

"But listen to me and listen good because I'm only gonna tell you this once."

"I'm listening."

"You are not to have a baby shower or a gender reveal party."

"But it's my—"

"I don't care if it's your first child. It's my tenth and I'm the one who's gonna be giving you money to support the two of you like I did with all of the other ones before you, so you do as I say.

"I don't find baby showers, gender reveal parties, push presents, and all of that other crap necessary. I think they're a waste of money when you don't need to have a party and gifts especially when you're saying this child is mine—and I believe you for right now but I still want the DNA test done—because it will have a great life all because of me. The most important thing of all is a healthy child and people lose sight of that because they get so wrapped up in all of that other shit."

She was crushed. "Okay, I understand."

"Oh, and you're not to have any more kids by any other man. Once you have a child by me then every man is off limits to have another child by. I told the other four the same thing, and yes, that does include my ex-wife because I know she's out there fucking other men now. I'm not paying for another child by you that's not mine, because I know there's no other men out there that any of you would have another child by that will have more money than what I have."

"I know they won't. And I wasn't going to."

"You better not. I'm serious." He took another sip of his drink. "Anything else you wanna say?"

Here was her time to ask him about the ring she'd found that she thought was her engagement ring.

"Um..."

He looked at her. "What is it?"

"Um...nothing," she said.

"Okay, then you can leave. I wanna be alone now."

"Okay," she replied in a disappointing tone.

Minutes later she drove home crying. *Well, I told him...about me being pregnant so there was no need for him to know about a ring he never knew I saw that I thought was an engagement ring. What I told him was more important anyway by far,* she thought, as she continued to sob.

CHAPTER FORTY-FIVE

One Year Later

The first-and-only child of Lisa was now three-month-old Kristianna Belle, and she was confirmed through DNA to be the tenth child of Nigel as well as his fifth daughter, so Lisa was confirmed to be the fourth baby mama. Five boys, five girls, one ex-wife, and four overall baby mamas. Lisa was now officially a part of all of the ongoing Nigel Foreman drama, but he did live up to his promise of taking care of them all.

Lisa still lived in the same house which was now hers since she officially bought it from her parents since Nigel told her he was not buying her a new house because he didn't buy any of the other baby mamas a house, and she was able to pay the monthly mortgage on it because of the overly generous amount Nigel gave her monthly for their baby, and the house was completely made over and furnished with some of the finest of furnishings; and it showed Nigel's wealth all on the inside as well as the outside. The baby had everything she needed in the three months she was here already and would always be taken care of, and Lisa couldn't be happier.

She sat on the couch as she breastfed her while Chassy and Sharita helped clean up the house. "Thank you for helping me out. Being a new mom is so exhausting and definitely life-changing that I haven't had time to do the simplest things anymore. I even had to quit school for right now because I just don't have the time to study. I'm glad I got people who really care about us."

"Well, you know we both know how it is to be a mom many times over, Lisa. You've got a beautiful baby girl and her father obviously loves her and takes care of her. *And* you got some expensive stuff in this house!" Chassy said.

"Yeah, I noticed it as well," Sharita said. "I guess not having a baby shower was worth it when you knew you can get all of these things for yourself and for the baby."

"Well, he gives me more than what I actually need because of the money he makes. His ex-wife and the other baby mama Haniah get a lot of things as well. Taylor's parents and Ivy's parents receive money from him as well for the kids neither one of them can take of anymore."

"Damn, that's still fucked up that Ivy did that shit. And she got fifty-plus years for it, too, with only a small chance of parole? She's probably never getting out," Chassy said.

"And that's her fault," Sharita said.

"Well, I don't have anything to do with what happened between the two of them. All I know is that me and my baby are being taken care of by Nigel as well and that's all I want and that's what I'm getting."

"Are you sure that's *all* you want?" Chassy asked.

Sharita looked at Lisa to see what she was going to say.

"Well, of course I want a serious relationship with Nigel, but at this point I just don't think it's gonna happen. We still see each other and everything, but he's always gonna do what he wants to do. It's too bad we haven't even been boyfriend/girlfriend now especially since we have a baby together, but neither Taylor, Ivy, nor Haniah was ever his girlfriend as well. But I still have a feeling he'll come around about it and when he does then hopefully I'll finally get that ring I thought I was gonna get over a year ago."

Chassy and Sharita looked at each other, and then continued cleaning up.

"But Kristianna is my biggest priority right now and forever will be. She's the love of my life. I don't think I ever really knew what deep and meaningful true love really was until I had her. I didn't even think about me being a divorced, single mom with a child not by my ex-husband, but by another man I was seeing all the time while I was still married and I ended up getting pregnant by him *after* my divorce. Sometimes things just don't work out like the way we want them to, but the bottom line is that I have my baby and that's all that matters to me."

Chassy and Sharita smiled at her.

"Yeah, that's all that mattered to us as well when we had our children, but it would've been nice to have been married before we carried," Sharita said.

"Yeah, really!" Chassy said with a laugh. "I learned my lesson from being a baby mama all right!"

"Well, I was married but never carried, but we tried. I just don't think having a child was meant to be between Greg and me other-wise I truly feel that it would've happened, but as you see it was meant to be between Nigel and me."

"Does Greg know about you having a child by Nigel?" Chassy asked.

"He has to know by now since she's three months. I posted a ton of pics on social media of her and everything, and he still follows me so I know he's probably seen them."

"You're not doing that to make him jealous, are you?" Sharita asked.

"No, absolutely not. It's my account so I can post whatever I want just like how anyone can. It's not like I got pregnant by Nigel when I was still married to him and tried to pass the baby off as being his knowing that it was Nigel's. I have a clean slate so I have nothing to feel guilty about."

"That's true, Lisa," Chassy said. "I just hope no one makes you feel bad about having your baby because people did that with me as you know."

"Me too," Sharita replied with her head down.

"Well, not everyone is gonna be happy for us, and we can ask any woman that. I think my parents weren't a hundred percent happy that I had a baby by Nigel because they expected for me to still have been married to Greg, but they love their granddaughter as if I am still married. I'm not gonna let people shame me for this. I don't believe in abortion and it's always my right to have a child if I want to just like it's a woman's right to get an abortion if she wants. And like I said before and I'll keep saying it, it was meant to be between Nigel and me, one day he'll see."

Chassy and Sharita once again looked at each other and shook their heads with a grin.

"She's delusional!" Chassy mouthed to Sharita; she laughed in response.

CHAPTER FORTY-SIX

"Lisa, I don't mean to interrupt you with whatever you were doing with the baby," Sharita said.

"Oh, I'm actually just watching TV since she's sleeping. What's going on?" Lisa replied, as Kristianna slept in her arms.

Sharita sighed. "Lisa, you're not gonna like this."

She sat up. "Not like what, Sharita? What's going on?"

"Apparently you haven't been on social media lately."

"No, I haven't been on it that much at all like the way I used to since Kristianna was born, why?"

"Well, one of my co-workers sent me this picture that I'm just gonna send to you."

"Okay."

Seconds later she got the picture on her laptop . . .

With Nigel smiling proudly with another woman as she flashed the 15-carat diamond ring!

"Hello? Lisa?"

"Yeah, I'm here," Lisa said as tears welled up in her eyes. "I'm trying to stay as calm as I can because I'm holding my baby and she's sleeping very well right now."

"Look, Lisa. Everyone told you Nigel wasn't any good. It's clear that he's been seeing this woman for a while since he gave her the ring."

"That should've been mine!" she hissed. "Mine!"

"Lisa, calm down. Your baby will be able to feel your negative energy. They're smarter at those ages than people think."

"I can't help it, Sharita," she said as tears streamed down from her eyes and drops fell on the baby's blanket. "He just completely led me on only to turn around and ask another woman to marry him."

"This is weird, Lisa, because it didn't say anything about him asking her to marry him. I think he just gave her that ring as a gift or something. She would've said something about being engaged to him and he would've really said it. They both just said it was a special ring because she was special to him. That's one hell of a special ring!"

"This isn't funny, Sharita. I feel betrayed by him."

"I wasn't trying to be funny, Lisa, not at all. And if you're gonna be this upset about it then I suggest you talk to him about it because it's clear he has another interest now. We all warned you about giving him so many chances and look what happened? You ended up getting pregnant by him, having his baby when he already had nine other kids, and now it's clear that he's moved on from you and on to another woman. This is what men like him do, Lisa, and they have the wealth and power to do it. I hate to say this, but he never cared about you like the way you thought he did."

"Look, I don't need to hear this right now, okay?"

"If not now then when, Lisa? When? I think this is the perfect time to hear this, and I'm not the only one who feels this way and you know it." She sighed. "Okay, I'm gonna be as real as I've ever been with you but I want you to hear what I have to say because I'm only gonna say this once to you, and you can get mad and hang up on me all you want, but I think it's high time that this was said."

"What?" she asked with a sigh as her tears kept coming at a steady pace.

Sharita let out a huge sigh. "Okay, here it goes. You had all of the warning signs that Nigel was no good, yet still you ended your marriage to a great man for him with no guarantees of anything, Lisa. How could you do that? You yourself said Nigel said he was never getting married again, so what made you think he would change is mind because you were single once again? Huh?

"You were never even his girlfriend, but you had a baby by him thinking that he would marry you because of it? He fathered *four kids* outside of his marriage to Aisha and never married any of the three mothers because he would be a polygamist if he did that shit. One of them was really stupid and had *two* kids by him? And she's the one who ended up killing the first baby mama and I *still* think Nigel had something to do with it all. How dumb could she be? And don't get even me started on what you ended up witnessing that night on that deserted road. Nigel didn't care about you then, either, all he cared about was protecting his own money and had that shit pre-planned all along.

"You had it all with Greg, Lisa, you really did. No, he's not nearly as wealthy as Nigel and yeah, he cheated on you and you finally caught him and you cheated on him as well—but I believe he truly loved you unlike Nigel. We all fuck up in our lives, that's why perfection for any of us should not be in any of our vocabularies. Why you did what you did is only something you know. I hope you feel it was all worth it."

Lisa sighed as stared down at Kristianna, almost drenching her in her tears. "Are you done? Because I gotta go."

"I hope you're going to get some help, Lisa."

CHAPTER FORTY-SEVEN

With Kristianna in tow, Lisa calmed herself down enough to drive to Nigel's home to see what was going on in terms of his relationship with a different woman. She tried not to think about what Sharita had told her but couldn't get it off of her mind.

Before she approached the guardhouse leading into Nigel's guard-gated community, she saw a convertible Ferrari slowly come out of the exit.

It was Nigel and his new girlfriend!

She backed up fast and turned around and headed right towards them as he now flew down the street. She began violently honking her horn and flashing her lights since it was dusk dark—she wanted him to know that she was trying to get his attention . . . .

But Nigel kept driving . . . and didn't stop until he reached the hotel and casino he was going to with his new girlfriend.

Lisa watched from her SUV as Nigel pulled up to the valet and got out of the car as his new girlfriend got out on the other side. They met up with each other, kissed, and then held hands as they walked into the main entrance.

Several minutes later, she walked fast and hard through the casino as she rolled Kristianna in her stroller on her search to try and find a man who she knew Sharita was right about all along, but since they had a child together, everything now between the two of them took on a whole new meaning and was at a whole other level than it had previously been.

She spotted them in one of the luxury restaurants, and was standing right in front of their table less than a minute later.

Nigel and his new girlfriend stared at Lisa as if they didn't know her. She recognized his girlfriend as the same woman he was with at his party, a party he acted as if he didn't want to spend any time with her at.

"What?" Nigel asked her.

"What? *What*?! Don't sit there and act as if you don't know me, Nigel, especially since we have a child together!" Lisa said as she stared down at him.

His new girlfriend looked at Kristianna and sighed, and then turned her attention back to Nigel, as she ran her right hand through her long, natural dark hair. And Lisa noticed that the ring was on her *right* ring finger and not her left.

"And?" Nigel asked. "What are you doing stalking me? You got what you wanted and you're not getting any more than what you're getting, so I suggest you leave or I'm gonna have you forcibly removed."

"Why did you do this, Nigel, why? You know how much I liked you!"

"This is not the time and place to talk about this, Lisa. What's done is done between us and you know it. I never told you to do any of the things you did, and you know what I'm talking about. Like I said, you've got you wanted and you're not getting any more than what you're getting, so if that's what you came here to talk to me about and to try and embarrass me in front of my girlfriend then it didn't work."

Lisa shook her head as tears began to well up in her eyes, and she tried her hardest to fight them back. "All I wanted was respect from you, Nigel."

"You're getting respect because of what you're getting monthly. Don't bother me about anything else or I'll rescind everything," he warned.

She knew it was no use in trying to talk to him anymore. She finally saw him for who he really was all along. She didn't wanna admit how right Sharita, Chassy, her parents, and everyone in her life who truly loved and cared about her were. She looked behind her and saw Russell staring at her as if he was waiting for Nigel to tell him to remove her from the restaurant. He looked like a whole different person to her now, and she was reminded very fast of what he did to Pierce Tatum on that deserted road because he wouldn't leave Nigel alone. She finally decided to turn around and walk calmly out of the restaurant on her own with her daughter as the tears flowed from her eyes.

Lisa sobbed as she stared at Kristianna as she slept soundly in her bassinette as she wrote in her diary:

> I confronted Nigel at a fancy restaurant that he was at with his new girlfriend, a girlfriend he acted as if he didn't wanna tell me about; a girlfriend who was wearing the ring that I discovered over a year ago in the drawer of his private room on his private jet. But what I thought was actually very interesting was that she was wearing the ring on her *right* ring finger, not her left one, so it's clear that he's not engaged to her, but he obviously thought she was special enough to give that ring to instead of me. I honestly don't know how long he's been seeing her, and I really don't care.
>
> I also didn't like the fact the he didn't even look at our

daughter while I stood there at their table and confronted him about our relationship, and I felt he totally disrespected her and me as her mom; even accused me of stalking him and said that he was gonna rescind the money he agreed to give me if I didn't leave him alone. I also didn't like the way his new girlfriend looked at my daughter as well, like she was disgusted at her presence since she was the current girlfriend of him now, and I was just some thot baby mama. But being his girlfriend was something I never was. I can imagine what he's told her about me, especially after I left.

I saw firsthand just the kind of person he's been all along. This is what happens when you let insanity take over your mind in thinking that someone is gonna change and giving them so many undeserving chances and they don't because they are who they are and I knew that about him all along. We have a child together and he's treating me as if I'm his enemy. It's not right at all because like it or not, we have a lifelong bond now and there's nothing any of his little girl-friends or him or anyone else can do about it.

CHAPTER FORTY-EIGHT

Two Days Later . . .

Lisa was jolted out of a deep sleep at the pounding on her front door more than the pounding of the rain coming down hard outside, combined by the constant ringing of her doorbell. She got up as Kristianna cried as she laid on the floor in front of her.

"What?! Who the fuck is banging on my door like this? What the hell?! SHUT UP!" she said, and swung open the door to Chassy and Sharita standing before her. They rushed inside.

"Oh, my God, Lisa! We've been trying to get in touch with you for over an hour now!" Chassy said, as she took her wet shoes off.

"Why? What is all of the banging at my door and constantly ringing of my doorbell about? The two of you never act like this!" Lisa said, and walked towards the family room where Kristianna was crying.

"Lisa, you know we wouldn't have rushed over here if it wasn't something we had to tell you in person," Sharita said.

"Because it's clear you haven't heard," Chassy said.

"Haven't heard what?" Lisa asked, as she picked up Kristianna to try and stop her from crying.

Chassy and Sharita looked at each other.

"Nigel is dead," Chassy informed her.

Lisa stood stunned. She literally couldn't move while Kristianna squirmed and cried in her arms. "Stop lying, Chassy," she calmly said.

"Lisa, she's not lying. It's been everywhere," Sharita said, and took Kristianna from her. "Sit down, you're in shock."

Chassy helped her sit down on the couch. "Lisa, he was killed in a plane crash this morning coming back from a business trip. They said it went down in bad weather. You see how it is out here right now. Everyone on the plane was killed."

Sharita sat in a reclining chair with Kristianna as she still cried. "You obviously haven't been looking at your phone."

Chassy grabbed Lisa's phone off of the end table and turned it on, and gave it to her so she could see for herself as all of the messages came down:

HIGH-NINE-FIGURE MAN NIGEL FOREMAN KILLED IN PLANE CRASH

NIGEL FOREMAN, KNOWN AS THE HIGH-NINE-FIGURE MAN, KILLED IN PLANE CRASH EARLY THIS MORNING ALONG WITH NINE OTHERS

NO SURVIVORS IN NIGEL FOREMAN PRIVATE PLANE CRASH

The messages would not stop coming.

"Lisa, look at me," Chassy said.

Lisa continued to stare at the wall in front of her that had a picture of her and Kristianna on it.

"Things like this don't happen every day when it comes to airplanes. This was clearly an accident. The best thing you can do is offer the Foreman family condolences and try to work out something with them when it comes to your daughter. She's too young to know what happened, and just because her dad isn't here anymore does not mean she shouldn't be taken care of by his surviving family as well. I know they're grieving right now, but I know you'll know when the time is right to talk to them. Get a lawyer if you have to because you're entitled to support for your child," Chassy said.

Lisa continued to stare at the wall in front of her as the cries of Kristianna echoed throughout the house. It was as if she knew what'd happened.

"I'll make us all some coffee," Chassy said, and got up.

"Lisa," Sharita said.

Lisa *still* continued to stare at the wall.

"I'm sorry this happened, okay? Like Chassy said, this was clearly an accident. Our first priority is that you and Kristianna are well cared for, and I agree with how you should have a meeting with the surviving Foreman family members to discuss getting some kind of child support from them since he's no longer here to give it. I know you told me you never legally put him on child support because he told you not to due to the fact that he could afford to support Kristianna, but you need to get something legal now that he's gone, Lisa. You need to do this for Kristianna."

Chassy sat back down after making the coffee. She turned on the TV to the news and to no surprise, it was their top story that they still had as Breaking News:

"We're following up on the Breaking News we brought you earlier today about the tragic, sudden death of the man who was known as the High-Nine-Figure Man, Nigel Foreman. We have a very partial list of who was on the plane with him this morning, and it reads as follows:

Nigel Foreman, 40
Russell Stymie, 42
Tanisha Takada, 38

"There were ten total, including the two pilots, one flight attendant, and four other passengers who we were told worked for Nigel at more than one of his businesses. We were also told that Tanisha Takada was the girlfriend of Nigel, and Russell was his close friend as well as personal bodyguard. We'll bring you more information as soon as it becomes available," the anchorwoman said.

The crashing sound of thunder shook the house, and Kristianna screamed in tears. Sharita gave her back to Lisa who still hadn't said a word.

The doorbell rang.

"I'll get it," Chassy said.

Seconds later, she walked back into the family room with Lisa's parents.

"Baby, we're so sorry," her mom said, as her dad nodded with his head down in agreement.

Tears began to stream from Lisa's eyes as they came over to her and consoled her.

CHAPTER FORTY-NINE

It was three weeks later, and Lisa opened the front door to her home and found Detectives Webber and Arnez standing in front of her. She tried not to go into a panic.

"Hello, Lisa. We just wanted to stop by to give you an update on the Pierce Tatum case," Webber said.

"Okay," Lisa replied, as she still stood in the doorway.

"Can we come in?" Arnez asked.

"Um, yeah, sure," she replied, and led them to the family room.

They sat down on the small couch and she sat in the reclining chair.

"First of all, we wanna extend our condolences on the loss of Nigel Foreman," Webber said.

"Thank you," Lisa said with her head down. "But I'm just one of moms of one of his surviving children."

"We know," Arnez said. "But we're not here about that, we're here because we wanted you to know that since Nigel's death, we went through some of his cars that were registered to him and found Pierce's DNA on the passenger's side of an SUV, and a Russell Stymie's DNA on the driver's side along with blood stains in the back seat, and the blood did match Pierce. Also, we found a gun inside of the glove compartment of the SUV as well. The ballistics report came back and told us that the bullets found in Pierce were definitely fired from the gun we found in the SUV. So, since Russell was killed in the plane crash along with Nigel then we're concluding that he's Pierce's killer, so the case is officially closed."

She wanted to breathe a big sigh of relief in front of them, but knew she had to contain her composure. "I'm glad you were able to solve the case."

"Did you know Russell?" Webber asked.

"No, I didn't," she lied.

"Well, it doesn't matter now. We also believe Nigel could've had something to do with it as well, but we never had the proof and now we can't do anything if he had something to do with it since he's dead as well. Did he ever tell you he had something to do with Pierce's murder?"

"No, he didn't tell me anything," she lied.

Webber and Arnez gave each other a skeptical look, and then looked at her.

"Lisa, if he did then you can tell us. You're not gonna get in any trouble," Arnez informed her.

Yeah, right, she thought. "I'm not lying. Look, I'm not trying to sound insensitive, but so much as happened in these past few weeks and it's still very hard for me to take it all in and I think it always will be, and it's affected a lot of people and it will affect us for the rest of our lives. I have to raise my daughter by myself now and she's only a little less than four months old now. I'm glad you guys were able to solve the case."

"So are we. Well, that's all we wanted to tell you. We'll see ourselves out," Webber said.

Later on that night, she received a text:

Hi, is this Lisa Everett?

Yes, this is Lisa. Who is this?

Hi, Lisa. I'm Haniah Knicks, I'm Nigel's third baby mama. I wanted to know if I could talk to you alone sometime this week?

Of course, Haniah. I look forward to it. I think we need to talk especially with everything that has gone on in these past few weeks.

We do, Lisa. I think it's been long overdue. I have so much I need to tell you and you don't wanna miss what I have to say.

And I look forward to it. Can't wait.

CHAPTER FIFTY

"Honestly, Haniah, I still can't believe Nigel is gone. I don't think I'll ever fully get over the shock of it. I literally couldn't talk when my best friend and cousin came over here and told me," Lisa said, as she sat a plate of fresh fruit on the kitchen table and sat down across from her.

"I know what you mean, Lisa. The first thing I thought about was my son. I couldn't think about anything else. Nigel provided very well for him and for the two of us, and I know he did the same in just a little over the three months you've had your child."

"Yeah, he did. It was a lot money just in those three months, enough where I was able to furnish this whole house with nice stuff as well as get Kristianna everything she needed. But now I admit I'm scared, Haniah. I just don't know what to do now. I took my friends and family's advice about reaching out to the Foreman family to offer my condolences and to talk to them about continued support for Kristianna, but no one from his family has responded to me. It's like they just don't care. I know they're still grieving right now and we are as well because we each have a kid by him, but I would think they would respect the fact that I would like to talk to them even though it's clear that they're disrespecting me by not even responding to me."

"That's how they are, Lisa, I hate to tell you that. They're assholes, to put it blunt. Nigel's parents, all of them. They only care about the kids he had with Aisha. You see how none of us were invited to his funeral because it was private. The family even said they didn't want us or his out-of-wedlock children there, my lawyer told me."

"That's not right at all!" Lisa replied, as she tried not to get angry.

"No, it's not, but it is what it is. Listen, I don't ever wanna say that my child was a mistake; it was just a mistake of who I had him by. But I learned my lesson from it and knew I had to move on when it was clear Nigel was not gonna leave Aisha for me—and why would he? I knew he was married to her and also knew he'd fathered three kids out of wedlock by two different women before me and never left his wife for either one of them, so what made me think he was gonna leave his wife for me? What made me believe I was so different, you know?"

Lisa lowered her head as she tried to choke back the tears that were welling up in her eyes. "And I thought just like you. I thought I was gonna be different from the three of you. And the second baby mama killed the first because she felt that since she had two kids by him that she was more special to him than the first one and deserved more *and* him as well since he was officially divorcing Aisha—but he wasn't divorcing her for her, that's what she failed to understand; what *I* personally failed to understand. I did think I was something special to him just like all three of you before me."

"We all thought we were special to him, Lisa. Hell, Aisha wasn't even special to him that's why they were getting a divorce, so what made any of us think we were? I hate to damn him in death, but Nigel cared about no one but himself and his businesses and lifestyle —and now he can't care about anything anymore. He left behind a big mess. A big, big, fat-ass mess. But I've officially taken myself out of it."

She looked at her as she wiped tears from her eyes. "What do you mean?"

"It means that I'm officially moving on like I told you a few minutes ago. I'm engaged to a Ghanaian man and we're getting married in Ghana . . . and we're staying there. He said he knew it was meant to be between us when I told him my name was Haniah, he said it's Ghanaian meaning of happiness and bliss, and he's surely given me and my son that. He's already accepted my son as his and wants to make things official between us. This is a chance for me to build a whole new life with someone who really loves and cares about me and my child, and Nigel was not that person. My fiancé is nowhere near as wealthy as Nigel was, hell, he doesn't even make six figures a year, but I'm happy, we're happy. Yeah, I thought I deserved a man like Nigel just like Taylor and Ivy did, but he was only married to one person, and it wasn't any of us. Honestly, Lisa, I wish I never met him."

"And it wasn't me, either," she said, referring to her never being his wife, and now she would never be. She shook her head. "The idea of marriage never came up when I told him I was pregnant, and I was too scared to ask him about it because I'd been married before and so had he."

"And just like Taylor, Ivy, and me, he was still legally married when you had your child by him."

Her mouth dropped in shock. "What?! *What*?! I thought he was officially divorced?!"

Haniah shook her head as she stared down at her coffee cup. "He never divorced her, Lisa. I had my lawyer check it out. He also had a will, of course, and it didn't include my child, nor Ivy's children, nor Taylor's child in it—just the ones that he had by Aisha. And I hate to tell you, Lisa, but it didn't include your child by him either. Apparently, the will was written before Taylor's child was born and he never changed it and never had any intentions on changing it, so it stands where it stands.

"Aisha is still legally his wife so she gets his entire estate, all high-nine figures of it, and my lawyer already told me that she doesn't want any of us contacting her in person or through social media or online or calling or texting or emailing her—*nothing*—about money for our children by him because we're not getting another dime. She also said what was given to us by Nigel was given to us and that's all that will ever be given to us since he's dead and that we should've been wiser with the money we were lucky to get from him.

"She also told her lawyers to tell my lawyer as well as Ivy's lawyer and Taylor's parents' lawyer that she will file a restraining order against us if we contact her in any way about support for our children and have us thrown in prison like Ivy, and she brought you up in it as well even though you don't have a lawyer; said you'll get the same as me and Taylor's parents if you contact her."

"And I thought she was a genuinely nice woman. Wow, how people really show their true colors in these types of situations, and I can't say I blame her, though. But I thought her and Nigel were legally divorced when I had my child by him because I was legally divorced. I can say that with a clear conscience."

"I know, Lisa. I believe you a hundred percent. That's how deceiving and conniving Nigel was. This is why I knew I should've went with my instincts and legally put him on child support, but I never did since I was getting money from him on a regular basis. Ivy never put him on it, either, and neither did Taylor when she was alive because they also received money on a regular basis from him, and as we all knew, what he gave us monthly was a lot of money where we could live off of it for well over a month."

Lisa was speechless. Her head continued to hang low. Her story, and all of the baby mamas before her, were exactly the same when it came to him telling them not to put him on child support because he could afford to support the kids he made, but what no one saw coming was what'd happened to him.

"Lisa, look at me."

She barely lifted her head.

"I know how much this hurts. Nigel hurt a lot of people, but Taylor, Ivy, and me allowed ourselves to be hurt by him. We all knew he was married at the time we had our affairs with him which resulted in us all having a child by him, but Taylor had one by him and she's dead—killed by Ivy who had two kids by him. Taylor's dead, Ivy's in prison for the next fifty years for killing her, Nigel is also dead so he can't cause any more of a mess than he's caused . . . and I'm moving on. I just can't with any of this anymore. The best thing you can do is find a great man and move on as well because at this point, we have no choice in the matter. Good luck."

CHAPTER FIFTY-ONE

Greg opened the front door to the home he used to share with Lisa as she stood looking pitiful before him while holding Kristianna. "Lisa, what are you doing here? Do you still have something in this house you forgot about? Because it's been well over a year since you've lived here."

"No, I haven't forgot about anything, Greg. I came over to talk. Do you have time?"

"I got time, Lisa, but not for you," he informed her.

She almost gasped. "Greg, I know I fucked up, okay? I just thought we could talk."

"There's nothing to talk about anymore, Lisa. And you fucking up is one of life's biggest understatements."

She sighed, and didn't wanna argue about how much he did the same. "Can I come in so we can talk?"

"No, you can't. You're my ex-wife, you no longer live here, and it's clear that you wanna talk about getting back together since your former lover is dead and you clearly thought you were gonna live the fairytale lifestyle with him once you divorced me and especially since you had a kid by him. At this point, Lisa, you should thank God that you're still alive and not Tanisha Takada that he dogged you for who was killed in that plane crash right along with him."

She sighed once again as she tried to suppress the tears that were welling up in her eyes as she adjusted Kristianna in her arms. "I didn't come here to talk about Nigel."

"Why not? He's the reason why you're standing here with his baby in your arms. It's because he's dead and now you want to return to me with a kid that's not by me because you finally realize you were wrong for what you did. Well, sorry, honey, but you don't get a do-over, especially since you're a single mother. He left you like the way he left all the others, and you should know by now that you're no different from them, and never were. At least those other three didn't divorce their husbands to be with him since they were all single."

"Greg, I didn't divorce you for him, *I didn't!*"

"I don't believe that one single bit, Lisa. Not one single bit. You can say it was because you caught me in the act of cheating on you, and that gave you the perfect reason to file for divorce even though you cheated on me as well. You needed something to mask the real reason you divorced me and that reason was to be with Nigel, and you got it, but you never officially had him, did you? Now Nigel's dead, you're left with a child you had by him, and you're trying to get your ex-husband back as if I'm just gonna forgive and forget."

She sighed once again. "Everyone makes mistakes and deserves a second chance."

"Not with me you don't, Lisa. I don't feel a bit sorry for you because of everything that has happened since you met that man. You had me, and you gave me up because you thought you would have a better life with him, now he no longer has a life and you're left to explain all of this to the kid you had by him."

A woman appeared at the door holding a newborn baby in her arms. Lisa did a double-take . . . .

It was Kayla Scott!

Nigel's half out-of-wedlock sister she spoke to about him well over a year ago.

"Lisa, hi! How are you?" she asked in a surprised tone.

"Go back in the family room. I'm talking to her," Greg said, and then stepped out of his house and closed the door behind him as Kayla still stood in the doorway. "See, I told you I wasn't gonna hold out any hope that you would change your mind about divorcing me."

"*Kayla Scott*, Greg? Really? Of all people? You knew I knew her."

"And she turned out to be a nice person when we hooked up after officially meeting each other on a dating site. We got married within a few months after meeting each other. Like I said, I wasn't gonna wait for you, Lisa, and I meant what I said. You hurt me beyond words with what you did, but as you see, I clearly moved on. I love Kayla and I love our son. Unlike you, she's a real one who appreciates the life that I've given her and hasn't tried to find someone who can give her a better one because unlike you she's not bored and lonely and doesn't take anything or anyone for granted. You need to learn from her, or you should've learned from her since she did tell you her story. Now this is the last time I wanna see you, Lisa, and I mean it, so get off of my property. I can't stand looking at you or at a baby that should've been ours."

After getting home from trying to talk to Greg, she wrote in her diary as Kristianna slept quietly next to her:

I had a great life, and I left it all for greed and uncertainty. I left a man who was good to me—but of course not perfect but who truly loved me unconditionally—for one who had more money, power, privilege, and prestige . . . one who had absolutely no interest in getting remarried . . . and I knew this. One who never divorced his wife . . . and I *never* knew this . . . now one who no longer has a life.

I was warned, warned by many people. Warned when I still

had a great life. A life most people would've wanted, a life I took for granted.

I have nothing now but a daughter out-of-wedlock and a heart that is smashed in a million pieces. My daughter doesn't have a father when she could've had one had I stayed married to Greg—but it's too late now. Greg has a new family of his own, something he wanted with me but I wasn't sure if I wanted it with him. He hates me, and rightfully so. I know more people hate me for what I've done and I can't blame them one single bit, even though they try and act like what I did was not as bad as it could be.

I know my family and friends are very disappointed in me, and I don't blame anyone for any of this but myself because no one wanted me associating with Nigel, no one, but I was the only one who couldn't see it because his status blinded me into a deluded fantasy to which I thought was gonna become a reality . . . and it never did.

I don't think Nigel ever had a true interest in me, it was just his ego that wanted to keep me around to serve his needs and his needs only, knowing that whenever he told me some-thing I wanted to hear it would make me feel better, more special, more wanted . . . and yeah, it worked, because I would like him even more so therefore I would graciously give him what he felt he needed without any question. He always knew how to pull me right back to him, right back into that fantasy, but—

This is the reality:

Nigel is dead.
Nigel never divorced his wife.

Nigel left behind ten kids and only five of them are officially
protected for life, and my daughter is not one of them.
Nigel will never give me any more money for anything.
I will never live the life I thought I was gonna live with him.

The only thing I feel I have moving forward is my daughter,
and raising her to be a beautiful, respectable woman. Exactly
like I *was* raised. But somewhere along the way I let an alter-
nate reality consume my every thought and emotion when
there was nothing wrong at all with the reality that I was
living in, and let myself get way in too deep with a man who
never gave a fuck about me and no one else but himself.

Now he can't even care about himself anymore.

I don't want my daughter being anything like the woman I
became, and I will regret my choices for the rest of my life.
The only hope I see is all in her, and it's up to me to be able to
raise that hope into something beautiful, something to live
for. I don't feel I made a mistake by having her, just who I had
her by. But it's *my* mistake, not hers, and she's not gonna be
the one subjected to people's nastiness because of it. I'll
protect her at any cost, something that her father failed to do
for her.

Now he can't do anything for her or for anyone anymore.

I was once a woman that women wanted to trade places
with, and now I became a woman that had her life replaced
by a woman who wished she was in my place . . . and now
she is. Unbeknownst to me at the time, I gave her my life, and
it's no one's fault but mine.

My life is nothing like what it used to be, and like I've said a million times, it's all my fault. Sometimes we have more than one life's lesson, and this is mine.

Lesson learned.
Lesson learned.
LESSON. LEARNED.

ABOUT THE AUTHOR

Sheila Murdock is a combination of her birth name and her late grandmother's maiden name on her mother's side. When she's not writing, she enjoys watching movies and TV shows - old and new - on YouTube, Netflix, and Amazon Prime Video, but always loves a surprising show she can find on cable TV. She also enjoys reading all kinds of non-fiction, but has a particular interest in African-American historical and contemporary non-fiction, but will read an occasional fiction book. She enjoys listening to old-school/throwback rap, hip-hop, and R&B, and jazz music from any era.

www.ingramcontent.com/pod-product-compliance
Lightning Source LLC
Chambersburg PA
CBHW021427150726
47989CB00001B/145